DRIFTWOOD WAR

Volume Five
in the Driftwood Saga

JAMES DAVIDGE

Illustrations by Eric Jordan

BAYEUX

DRIFTWOOD'S WAR: *Volume Five in the Driftwood Saga*

Copyright © 2010 James Davidge, *text;*
Eric Jordan, *illustrations;* Fiona Staples, *cover illustration*

Published by: Bayeux Arts, Inc.,
119 Stratton Crescent SW,
Calgary, Canada T3H 1T7,
www.bayeux.com

Cover image: Fiona Staples
Illustrations: Eric Jordan

Library and Archives Canada Cataloguing in Publication

Davidge, James, 1973-

Driftwood's war / by James Davidge ; Eric Jordan, illustrator.

(Driftwood saga ; v. 5)
ISBN 978-1-897411-17-9

I. Jordan, Eric, 1973- II. Title. III. Series: Davidge, James, 1973- .
Driftwood saga ; v. 5

PS8607.A7748D746 2010   jC813.6   C2010-900539-2

First Printing: March 2010
Printed in Canada

Books published by Bayeux Arts/Gondolier are available at special quantity discounts to use as premiums and sales promotions, or for use in corporate training programs. For more information, please write to Special Sales, Bayeux Arts, Inc., 119 Stratton Crescent SW, Calgary, Canada T3H 1T7.

All rights reserved. No part of this publication may be reproduced, stored in a retrieval system, or transmitted, in any form or by any means, electronic, mechanical, recording or otherwise, without the prior written permission of the publisher, except in the case of a reviewer, who may quote brief passages in a review to print in a magazine or newspaper, or broadcast on radio or television. In the case of photocopying or other reprographic copying, users must obtain a license from the Canadian Copyright Licensing Agency.

The publishing activities of Bayeux/Gondolier are supported by the Canada Council for the Arts, the Alberta Foundation for the Arts, and by the Government of Canada through its Book Publishing Industry Development Program.

Canadian Heritage   Patrimoine canadien

Canada Council for the Arts   Conseil des Arts du Canada

Alberta Foundation for the Arts

For Christa

SPECIAL THANKS

to my daughter Ella Davidge
for calmly crawling at my ankles while I type,
to Natalie Norcross for her gracious editing,
to Jason Howse and Laurie Harris for
their insightful advance readings,
and to the students and staff at Willow Park
for their ongoing inspiration as
learners and teachers, all.

CONTENTS

I see the blood and lightening
Of heavy conflicts frightening

This violence of a vengeful trance
May vanquish if we launch to dance

Chapter One

RAVE OF THE GODS

There is a realm where light moves very slowly, oozing about its otherworldly dimension, like jellyfish traveling ocean water. Light, often believed to be faster than anything else in our universe, has inspired many scientific theories attempting to define its ambiguous nature. The Land of Crawling Light contradicts every single one of them. In this altered state the radiation of many wavelengths exists as cloudy shapes of solid, liquid and gaseous matter, making many forms, including gamma ray pillars and microwave mists. When this energy is moving at the speed of maple syrup pouring down a new shirt, one can sense that these waveforms are comprised of particles that are each fascinatingly distinct and very possibly alive.

Old Bart had only visited the Land of Crawling Light once before, when he was a much younger man. On both tours he traveled by astral projection, the practice of allowing one's soul to journey great distances away from its physical body through calm meditation. On this second encounter, Bart was thankful to be accompanied by his longtime friend Murph Magee, a knight and spy for the Order of the Good and True, who, due to many previous experiences in this bizarre realm, was demonstrating a greater comfort with the strange atmosphere.

"I'm feeling kind of soul-sick," complained Old Bart. "This is no place for a mortal like me."

"You should feel privileged," advised Murph. "The Bacchanalia only occurs in the Land of Crawling Light every six and a quarter centuries."

"It was partially because of ridiculous places like this that I moved to the quiet Arctic in the first place."

"Quit being such a senior. This event worked well for a quick meeting because the Seer's translator is from this realm."

The two men were floating around the fringe of a giant party of mystics, immortals and conceptual beings, most of whom were dancing to music emanating from blobs of radio waves that bounced about. Gods of tricks flirted with goddesses of sticks. Fairies hovered and boogied. Angels cavorted with demons. Feet, hooves, talons and tentacles stomped, tapped and slid on the hard x-ray floor. Eternal mingling occurred aplenty. Entities from components of every earthly or unworldly culture were represented somewhere in the quite powerful mishmosh.

Old Bart felt a massive hand firmly grip his shoulder. Reluctantly preparing for a confrontation, he started to scratch his nose, wondering if it was even wise for him to consider summoning lightening in such a luminescent realm. He turned to face his quarry. He quickly realized that he should have expected such a greeting.

"Ah! Strong sirs of the land of form, you have found us," bellowed Odin the All-Father. "It is good to see mortals so close to the end of their lives in such sturdy shape. Please join us at our table."

Old Bart relaxed somewhat.

"End of my life, eh?" he quipped. "How many times have you Viking gods died only to return again and again, bringing about

Ragnarök, an end of days, in some different form each and every performance?"

"Calm your friend, Sir Magee," Odin cautioned. "We're all allies here."

"Worry not, Odin," assured Murph. "Old Bart has spent the better part of the last thirty years in northern isolation. Public gatherings tend to make him uncomfortable."

Murph and Old Bart sat down at a table with a top that was sometimes a perfect circle and during other moments an irregular ellipse. Old Bart found himself beside a warrior woman clad in armour over a silk dress.

"I am Freya, leader of the ancient Valkyrie," she introduced.

"Madam, it is a sincere pleasure," Murph declared. "The glorious and graceful impact that the Valkyrie have had on the planet since their return has been most impressive. Perhaps that is why the Order wanted me to arrange this meeting."

"Why'd you bring your rude decrepit friend?" mused Odin.

"Careful, one-eye," warned Old Bart. "I sneeze and lightening bolts would explode out of your kneecaps."

"Again with your insolence! You are nothing

here, whelp, amongst gods and monsters."

The tension was fortunately interrupted.

"My master disagrees with you," hummed an irradiant voice, "and brings apologies for not being punctual but reminds you all to embrace slowness whenever possible."

The two old men and duo of gods were approached by a sentient ball of light that had just addressed them. Accompanying the sphere was a giant gorilla that held a silver serving tray. Murph paid respectful attention to the contents of the tray.

"May I humbly introduce everyone to the Seer of Eternal Beyonds," Murph said.

Bart began, "But you're a..."

"It knows what it is," the translator routinely explained, "and it's been the guiding prophet for the Order of the Good and True since long before you were born. Only Peter Z. Juice has greater authority."

"You're the prophet? When I was working for the Order I was following what you foresaw?" Bart clarified, staring at the silver tray with its banal contents.

There was a pause as translator and prophet communicated.

"Did it really feel like work to you?" the light

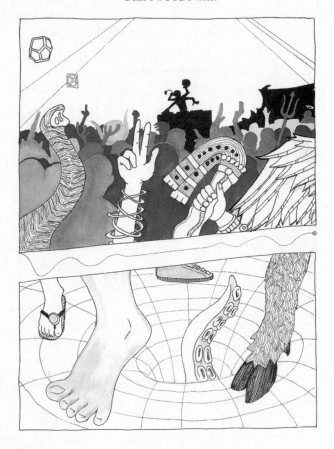

*Entities from components of every
earthly or unworldly culture were represented
somewhere in the quite powerful mishmosh.*

hummed. "Wasn't it more like an adventure?"

"The job came with risk, if that's what you mean, but it was still just a job."

It took a moment for a response.

"Why do you say that?"

"Because I was able to quit. A true adventure never really ends."

Another moment.

"Are you sure about that?"

"Finality is an illusion. Besides, if I recall, Murph had long ago told me that the Order was in support of my decision to quit being one of their knights."

"Of course," the Seer confirmed via the light.

"And why was that, if you don't mind me asking?"

"You had a greater destiny that only your settling on Ellesmere Island could fulfill."

"Do you mean raising and training Driftwood?"

"Perhaps."

"Well, thank you for being so ominously mysterious."

"Excuse me," Odin interjected, "but I am beginning to wonder why this gathering was called."

The light began to glow bright and flicker

slightly.

"Powers that have been at play for eons are about to culminate. Ancient forces are at work and they carelessly bring civilization to the brink of destruction. I come with advice that I urge you to heed. Odin, you have been fighting corporate-controlled giants on Earth."

"It has been a glorious battle as Thor, Baldar, Tyr and I thrash those supermarket-vomiting behemoths," confirmed Odin.

"My advice to you is to keep on that task. Ignore your son Loki's manipulations. Freya, you have become a politician in the country of Norway."

"I have been elected the leader of the Socialist Left Party. We currently share power with the Labour Party and the Centre Party."

"You will have to make sure that your parliament does not follow the sway of the sword. Remind them that it's only a small island."

"Can you be more specific?" asked Freya. "What island are you speaking of?"

"Bart?" the light said, ignoring Freya's query.

"Yes?" the curmudgeon responded.

"Protect the grandmother."

"Pardon me?"

"Sir Murph Magee?" the light again ignored the request for details.

"Yes, great Seer of Eternal Beyonds?" Murph responded, surprised that he was to receive a message. He thought his only duty was to call the meeting.

"You too have an important role."

"Really?"

"Get the kids to where they need to go."

"Huh?"

"That is all. We thank you for your time."

The gorilla jumped away, carrying with it the silver tray. The light entity followed closely behind, leaving Old Bart, Murph, Freya and Odin to contemplate their individual messages.

"That's it?" stammered Old Bart. "My soul traveled all this way to be personally told just three words by a fortuneteller on a plate? How am I even supposed to know which grandmother to protect? Do I just return to Ellesmere Island as planned or do something else? What do you have to say about that, Murph?"

Before Murph could answer, the group's table was knocked over by a tumbling brawl between an angel and a demon.

Chapter Two

WHAT'S IN A NAME?

"Ooomp!"

Driftwood had grown to love making that sound. It meant she was expressing a moment of pure strength and focus.

"Ah."

She also reveled in her relaxing exhales as her intensity would eventually dissipate and tranquility would wave over her with welcome.

"Ooomp!"

Focus.

"Ah."

Calm.

Driftwood was sitting cross-legged in the middle of the main field at Camp Magee with backs of hands on knees and fingers pointed up. Standing near her was Peter Z. Juice, leader of the Order of the Good and True, wearing a tuxedo that had been torn and burnt to shreds and ash. He was watching as two tiny robots each with six mechanical arms were hammering, welding and scrambling to repair Juice's nearly destroyed helicopter. Picking at a hole in Peter's left pant leg was Edie the Eaderion. Edie was Driftwood's pet, part lion, part eagle and part spider. It had eight furry legs with clawed paws, a bulbous body, great wings and a pinching beak. Edie suddenly took notice of a spectre floating towards them.

"Quite a ship Peter has," greeted the ghost, "and your pet is so marvelous."

"Hello, Mom," Driftwood returned as her eyes opened up.

Driftwood had recently returned from the forest planet of Atlutopia where she had been reunited with the ghost of Eva Wood, her mother. Eva, who was abused by her father, found herself pregnant with the child of her angry and violent husband, Hans Blekansit. She fled Blekansit Manor in the Caymon Islands and, fearing her family's house and the lash of her dad, Rotten Wood, she journeyed to the far north. Eva had died shortly after giving birth to Driftwood, leaving the baby girl to be raised by Old Bart and the staff of the Toque and Mitt Inn, near the Eureka Research Station on Ellesmere Island, the most northern island in Canada. They initially had shared corporeal existence for only brief seconds and, more than a decade and a half later, the two had grown close since traveling across the universe together.

"I want to come with you," Eva declared. "We're just getting to know each other."

"I'm sorry, Ms. Wood," explained Peter Z. Juice, "but the Order's headquarters is not easily endured by ghosts. You would most likely get compressed to nothingness."

"Mom?" Driftwood meekly called out.

"Yes, dear?"

"Something I've always wanted to know is why you named me Driftwood. It's a pretty strange birthname for anyone, let alone a girl."

"I was always very scared of my father," Eva confessed. "It wasn't until I ran away from his torturous treatment that I gained power over myself. It was the same when I realized I was in that horrible marriage with your father. I felt that the ability to leave a bad situation was a great skill. You're named Driftwood because I wanted to encourage you to wander. To drift, to

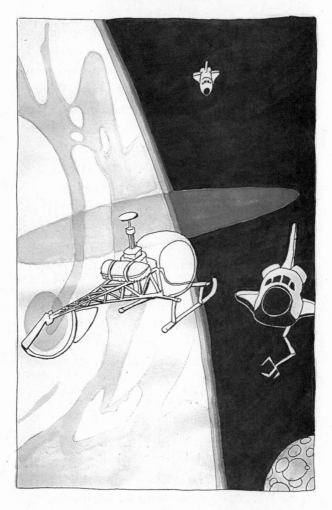

"Quantum moment!" commanded Peter.

travel, to float and, most importantly, to endure. Like the remnants of a formerly grand tree I wished for you to be shaped into something ornately beautiful and sublimely strong. What's amazing is you've grown up to become someone who runs towards problems, not retreat from them. You are much braver than I ever was."

"You traveled a long way from two cruel homes and found me a safe place to grow up. I got my courage from somewhere and it certainly wasn't from my father."

The two tried to hug but Driftwood's arms went through Eva's body. Mother floated away from daughter. Soon it was back to just Driftwood, Edie the Eaderion and Peter Z. Juice waiting in the middle of the field.

"How long until we go?" asked Driftwood, trying to ignore the tears that emitted from her eyes.

"The Pointed Feather will have healed itself in no time," explained Juice.

"Why won't you let me summon the Squamish Thunderbird or something to fly us there?"

"We prefer to be more diplomatic in our dealings with deities. If you view them as taxis then that is all they will be to you."

Driftwood felt like she was being lectured to. She never liked it when Old Bart did that. She liked it even less from the leader of the Order of the Good and True. She sat silently.

"So you've just learnt why you're called Driftwood," observed Peter Z. Juice trying to make conversation. "Do you know the history of the name Ellesmere?"

"I know that Ellesmere Island was named by its British discoverers after the Duke of Ellesmere," replied Driftwood, "who used to speak out in favour of child labour in factories. I helped his tortured spirit achieve redemption."

"But do you know the meaning of the word? What Ellesmere translates into?"

"I always thought it came from the French words *elle* and *mere*. I imagined it meaning *She-mother*. Like the opposite of *He-man* or something."

"Interesting deconstruction. However, the name actually comes from Olde English and means Ellis Pond."

"Ellis?"

"And Ellis is a version of Elijah."

"Elijah?"

"Meaning *God is the Lord* in Hebrew. The legend is that Elijah was a prophet in ancient

Israel and was part of the Temple of Jerusalem. Elijah and his supporters believed that all should worship only their god. For them, it was Yahweh or the highway. King Ahab and Queen Jezebel worshipped a god by the name of Baal and set up idols within the walls of the temple. Not since the days of Solomon had anyone been allowed to worship any but Yahweh within the temple. Elijah called forth for fire to destroy Ahab and Jezebel. The royal couple was burnt to oblivion amidst their monuments."

"I think I prefer my *She-mother* definition. Elijah sounds like he was a little intolerant."

"What you've said is perhaps a very fair and relevant assessment. Remember this lesson, Driftwood."

"I'm self-taught these days."

"We'll see about that. Now stand up. Our chariot awaits."

It had been slightly more than three hours since the Pointed Feather had crashed in a smoldering heap onto the field of Camp Magee, carrying Peter Z. Juice as its sole passenger. In that short time the obscurely shaped craft had entirely reconstructed itself and was now hovering above them, propeller blades casually turning, with a cable ladder hanging from an open door. Peter Z. Juice and Driftwood both stepped onto the bottom rung. As the ladder pulled them up, Edie the Eaderion flew alongside. Instantly, after the trio's secure entry, the craft ascended at an incomprehensible velocity. Peter slipped into a pilot's seat. Driftwood buckled herself in. Edie bounced about. Driftwood looked out the window and saw the scenery hastily change from sky to cloud to stars.

"Are we going into space?" she asked.

"To our secret headquarters," Peter Z. Juice confirmed.

"Uh, how can a helicopter fly into space? The propellers would need air to create an updraft."

"Oh the propellers are just to reduce undesired attention, however we do use the blades as solar panels for accessory power. The Pointed Feather's main fuel is an advanced anti-gravity fission propulsion system that combines technology and magic."

"Sir, we have a problem!" the front terminal buzzed. "Shuttles at twelve o'clock!"

Directly in front of them were two American spaceships. One was trying to grip the craft with a hydraulic arm. The other was releasing numerous payloads directly in front of the

Chariot's path which was about to crash into a movie channel satellite.

"Quantum moment!" commanded Peter.

The Feather blinked away only to reappear over a thousand kilometres further into space and well away from the meddling space shuttles.

"They won't be getting this far," assured Juice. "NASA spacecraft are currently very limited."

"Where are we going?" asked Driftwood. "The moon?"

"Much farther than that, to the fifth planet in our solar system."

"Jupiter? But isn't it made of gas?

"Only its outer shells are gaseous. We'll be traveling below the liquid metallic hydrogen layer towards its dense core."

"How will we get there?"

"By flying through the eye of the Red Storm, of course."

Chapter Three

"Mr. President, Juice's craft got away but we have been able to discern their trajectory," the Secretary of Defense nervously informed. "They may have given away the location of the Order's secret headquarters."

"And you're sure Driftwood was with Juice?" demanded Hans Blekansit, President of the United States, as he sat at his oval office desk while being surrounded by various advisors, a camera crew and a frantic director.

"Our source says she reappeared on Earth a few hours ago after being missing for almost a year. That was why Peter Z. Juice was returning to Earth when we first confronted him and shot him down."

"Where has she been?"

"On some forest planet or something."

"This will not do. Without her to antagonize me I've managed to become the most powerful man in the free world. Now she is in the sanctuary of my most hated enemies, the Order of the Good and True."

"Ten seconds until action, Mr. President," the video director said.

"I've worked too hard getting where I am to have it all ruined by my meddlesome teenage daughter."

"And three, two, one...action!"

"My fellow Americans, there is trouble brewing in the backyard we like to call Canada. They are in a dispute with Denmark over a little island in the north. Do you want to know what this place is called? Hans Island. Although only a coincidence, that title has warmed my heart. Both Canada and Denmark lay claim to this land. We shall support the Canadians and do whatever it takes to ensure their borders are thoroughly protected and established. Goodnight."

"And cut. Great work, Mr. President. Short, sweet and ominous. Your trademark."

"A few words to stir the pot were all that was needed. We'll be at war in no time. That little rock of an island is going to be great for business. When do I get to see our new toys, Mr. Secretary?"

"I'll prepare Air Force One for flying to Area 57 immediately, Mr. President."

The Secretary of Defense flinched and fled out of the oval office, followed quickly by the camera crew. Hans Blekansit pressed a button on his phone as if that was the only thing he was good at.

"Juanita, get me a peanut butter and shark sandwich," he commanded. "Also, send for the First Lady and my son."

"Your family is already here waiting for you, Mr. President," Juanita communicated through the telephone.

"Send them in."

Helena Betty Hayes Blekansit, clad in a pink dress with matching fashionable hat, and their son Harry Blekansit, sporting an expensive yet slightly tacky suit, both entered the room with bold swaggers normally reserved for only the extremely confident or newly and significantly empowered.

"Father, I've become so popular since becoming the President's son. I've given five televisions interviews this week," announced

Harry, "that were all about how I like to throw rocks at things."

"Isn't it great to see Harry back to his normal self again, darling?" Helena asked Hans. "I was worried that working out at Camp Magee may have given him some sort of heightened and dangerous concern for others."

"He's distinctly selfish. He'll be a great and powerful citizen," affirmed Hans.

"And I've never felt better. The White House does wonders for one's sense of self and general happiness."

"I'd be happier if I hadn't learnt that Driftwood has just returned."

"So your daughter's back from her journey, eh?"

"And what do you know about it, my wily wife?"

Helena had left Hans when Harry was very young. She had stolen the magical book of Heinz Blekansit, Hans's father, and used it to become a powerful sorceress. Recently reunited with Hans and Harry, she has since tried to kill Driftwood on more than one occasion.

"Same as you, my suspicious husband. Up near Camp Magee, I teleported her into a tree that inexplicably floated into the sky and then disappeared through a warped reality portal. No one has seen her since."

"So you've always said."

"I'm sensing some passive hostility and mistrust, Hans. Is there something you want to ask me?"

"Where have you been going? You're barely around."

"I told you. I have many charities and causes to attend to."

"But you never tell me what they are!"

A loud shatter disrupted the argument and the couple and their son all fell backwards trying to avoid a bolt of lightening that blasted through the window. As glass pieces fell to the ground, a dozen secret service agents ran into the room. They protected the First Family by throwing their own bodies in front of the shards. The men in black suits all stood up, allowing the debris to fall off their backs. One of them had been impaled and was whisked away by two others. The rest watched with Hans, Helena and Harry as the surge of electricity began to take on the physical form of a man. The creature had the features of a werewolf, only his skin glowed and he sported a fur of static and spark. The radiant beast startled everyone with a mighty howl, inviting the gunfire of the agents. They quickly stopped firing after realizing that bullets went right through the entity of electricity. Hans regained his composure and addressed the otherworldly invader.

"What in blazes are you?"

"I am Enkidu, of your ancestral past. I wish for you to lend me assistance in my long haunted goal."

"And what is that?"

"Revenge."

"Well, you sound like a Blekansit."

Chapter Four

Driftwood was feeling sick to her stomach. The Pointed Feather had already spiraled numerous times around the inner circumference of the crimson funnel cloud that led to the centre of Jupiter. The craft was still only on the outer edge of the planet's chaotic surface, where the Red Storm of Jupiter is at its most volatile. All around them gaseous substances vapourized and coagulated into nonexistent voids and crystallized globules. Bolts of sapphire lightening and translucent waves of red-shifted particles sparked and flowed in every direction.

"Eeeiii-whindy-windy-why?" squawked Edie.

"D-d-did you know J-j-jupiter could have been another st-st-star like the sun if its

m-m-mass had been only slightly l-l-larger?"
Peter bumpily lectured amidst the maelstrom.

"I can't think about that right now!"
Driftwood answered as she strained to
overcome her vertigo. Her abdomen muscles
clenched and tightened.

"B-b-brace yourselves. We are about to pass
through liquid hydrogen. You m-m-may feel
yourself g-g-getting a tad denser."

"I'm surprised the weight of gravity hasn't
crushed us entirely."

"Both the P-p-pointed F-f-feather and our
headquarters u-u-utilize dimensional warps to
shift the gravitational f-f-field around us."

"Sounds impossible."

"You'll g-g-get used to it. You already
ap-p-pear more comfortable with this than I
a-a-am."

"I've done a lot of space travel these days but
I'd be lying if I said I wasn't about to throw up."

Driftwood looked out a window. The
red sky had changed to an ocean of
sparkly metal that reminded Driftwood
of the mercury in the old thermostats at
the Toque and Mitt Inn. Whenever the
blob connected the circuit of two wires,
a blue spark would emit. Driftwood now watched

as a silver sea was embedded with streams of blue light that slithered about like electric blood vessels.

"Metallic hydrogen is a very special super-conductor," explained Peter as the ship started to slow down.

Driftwood looked out the front to see a giant translucent dome sitting on a now visible rocky surface. The hydrogen lapped against the dome in glittery waves. Inside was what looked like a wondrous stone and steel castle the size of a small village. The Pointed Feather landed on the top of the dome. The glass surface allowed the spacecraft to permeate through and soon Driftwood found herself flying above a forest of mechanical trees with girders for branches and aluminum panels for leaves. She watched as a massive drawbridge lowered and they flew into a grand courtyard.

Greeting them was a very tall man who was holding up a tuxedo on a hanger until the hook appeared to go right through his hand causing the suit to fall to the floor. The man struggled but eventually succeeded in again holding the suit in a distinguished manner.

"Who's that?" asked Driftwood.

"That's Gilgamesh," explained Peter. "He's

currently working as my servant."

"Is he all there?"

"What do you mean?"

"That suit's hanger just went through his hand."

"Gilgamesh used to be a ghost."

"Used to be?"

"The unique properties of Jupiter's core allow him to exist as a near physical being. He has served me for the last few weeks. I'm afraid it hasn't been going well. I hate wrinkly clothes."

"Then why have him serve you?"

"It is his penance by choice. He yearns to make amends for acts from long ago."

"What are you talking about?"

"You'll have to wait for your lessons to find out."

"Lessons?"

The door to the Pointed Feather opened.

"Welcome home, Sir Juice," greeted Gilgamesh with a bow. "I have your new clothes as requested."

Gilgamesh held up the tuxedo only to have it fall through both his arms onto the rocky ground.

"Not again," he muttered.

"Just bring it inside so I can get changed,"

instructed Peter Z. Juice, "and then go summon the faculty to meet their new student. Driftwood, please step off the ship so I can have some privacy."

"Student?" repeated Driftwood.

Moments later, a group of beings entered the courtyard. They arranged themselves around Driftwood just as the Pointed Feather's door re-opened to reveal Peter in a pristine outfit.

"May I present to you the four teachers of the Regimental Conservatory," he announced.

"Teachers?" returned Driftwood.

Her discomfort and confusion did not halt the introductions as Peter waved his hand in front of a cow that wore a gown and stood on two legs.

"This is the Sacred Cow," he explained, "who will teach you philosophy."

"Moo," said the Sacred Cow, "and Oom. All knowledge is balanced with mystery."

"And this is Michael Magee," explained Peter, "who just returned from an adventure in Dimension Zero."

"I almost learnt of its unknown origins," furthered Michael, a man in Khaki shorts, a safari hat and wielding a long staff, "but I found nothing."

"Are you Swamp's father?" inquired Driftwood.

"And Murph Magee's son," confirmed Michael. "I'll now be your history instructor."

"And this great being," continued Peter, "is the Seer of Eternal Beyonds, along with its carrier, Simia, and translator, Illumina. The Seer will teach you the prophetic arts."

"But it's a rock. On a tray. Being held by a gorilla," observed Driftwood. "Beside a glowing light."

"The Seer knows what it is," Illumina announced.

"One of your teachers is a stone?"

"The Seer of Eternal Beyonds helped me found the Order of the Good and True thousands of years ago" explained Peter. "It has much to teach."

"You were around thousands of years ago?"

"Last but certainly not least," Peter changed the subject, "is the Grand Cubile."

Driftwood was met by a hovering bee hive.

"Pleazed to meet you," buzzed the Grand Cubile. "I zhall teach you zkillz and rigour. Zhall we take you to your firzt clazzroom to meet the other ztudentz?

"Classroom? Students?"

"Of course, Driftwood," said Peter. "You have much to learn."

Driftwood already did not enjoy how school was making her feel like she didn't know anything.

Chapter Five

Dear Clov-ster,

*Wuz'up crazy lady? I still can't
believe that you're in Belgium. You're
becoming as adventurous as Driftwood,
who barely stayed to visit with the rest of
us. She went off with that Peter Juice dude
shortly after you went to the airport.*

*Swamp and Marsh and baby Meagan
are doing fine. Swamp is still able to run
Camp Magee and be a father at the same
time. Marsh tends to the horses while
being a mother. They're very busy people.*

*Your bro, Wave, is much appreciated
around here, especially for his humour.*

*Glacier is still as kind as ever. Lichen
keeps climbing higher mountains. And
Stormy is, well, Stormy. He's never really
been the same since he went traveling.*

*I'm having a blast. I recently invented
a new snack that involves chocolate chips,
bananas, chicken legs, goat cheese and paprika.
Kids only eat it on a dare. I've also taken to
reading the online international news now
that you are such a major player on that scene.*

*Have fun being a slave to global
governing systems, you crazy intern you.*

*Love,
Rose*

Clover gently folded the paper up and carefully inserted it into her inside jacket pocket. She had read the letter three times in the last hour. It was her first piece of mail she had received since starting her job as a page at the headquarters of the North Atlantic Treaty Organization in Brussels, Belgium. That made it very valuable.

Having previously held Canada's ambassadorship to Denmark, Clover's father had used some serendipitous diplomatic connections to ensure his daughter the much sought after position. After all the effort that had gone into getting her the job, Clover was surprised by how easy it was. She basically delivered little slips of paper from one person to another. It was explained to her that in the world of international peacekeeping, electronic devices such as telephones and the internet could sometimes not be trusted.

Clover entered into the largest meeting room of the NATO headquarters. In it were gathered delegates from all twenty-six of its member nations. This included representatives from Canada, the United States and most of the countries in Europe. Clover's job was to quietly pass along messages to specific delegates while the more public discussion was taking place. Clover's assignment was to deliver a message for the United States of America delegate. As she walked quietly, the public discussion continued at an intense level. The Secretary General, who happened to be from the Netherlands, was addressing the Canadian delegate.

"Mr. Mackenzie, it has been made very clear from his public statement that the President of the United States of America is supporting your country in some squabble with Denmark over a small piece of rock," the Secretary General announced. "Are you aware of the damage such a conflict could have to the integrity and security of our organization?"

"Mr. Secretary General and the delegates of our great sister countries," began Donald Mackenzie, "the nation of Canada was not expecting the Unites States to get involved so aggressively. Hans Island is a tiny island in our Arctic waters. It is our hope that we can resolve this issue amicably with Denmark and not cause disruption to the many treaties that keep this mighty peacekeeping organization interdependently entwined towards its humanitarian cause. Oh, excuse me."

Clover handed the Canadian delegate the slip of paper from the American delegate. He paused to read the message. Donald "Bug" Mackenzie was a former hockey player turned lawyer, turned politician, turned diplomat. After reading only a few short sentences silently to himself, his faced turned red, sweat began to emit copiously from his forehead and he resumed his speech in a monotone fashion, giving up any pretenses of autonomy.

"However, let it be known that if Denmark does not surrender its claim over Hans Island then Canada will have no choice but to engage the Danes in military action."

"Is that a threat?" responded the Danish delegate amidst the confused chatter of the other member delegates.

"Apparently so," Don Mackenzie meekly responded, realizing that his country was now part of a very dangerous game.

Chapter Six

BOYS AND THEIR TOYS

"You're my ancestor?" Hans Blekansit questioned the bestially electric being that had infiltrated the oval office.

"The first Blekansit was born of the union between myself and the beautiful priestess, Shamhat," Enkidu crackled in a growly voice. "After my untimely death before my child's birth, my soul traveled to the centre of our sun. For thousands of years, my spirit pushed through the great heat and fire to re-emerge as a being of pure energy. Riding a solar wind I journeyed to the closest planet and discovered two immovable monks named Ferreus and Porcus. Coincidentally, they knew of your existence and were able to discern the connection between us. After I road a solar flare to Earth, it did not take me long to find you."

Ferreus and Porcus were both eight-hundred year old merchant-monks who had helped Hans create Blekan-Mart vomiting giants. During an altercation with Driftwood and her friends, the pair had ended up frozen in time and banished to the planet Mercury.

"And what specifically do you want?"

"I have now returned to Earth after millenniums of purgatory and, with your help, hope to seek revenge against the best friend who betrayed me, Gilgamesh."

"Gilgamesh? Never heard of him. However, since I am the most powerful man on Earth, I'm sure I'll be able to help you out eventually. For now, we must go and inspect my weapons."

Enkidu followed Hans, Helena and Harry as they entered a helicopter and flew across the Potomac River to the Ronald Reagan Washington National Airport in Arlington, Virginia. They boarded Air Force One, the official Presidential plane, which took off immediately.

"Where are we going, Dad?" asked Harry.

"Area 57," replied Hans.

"Where's that?"

"Even I don't know. They use three different pilots along the way so that not one of them knows the whole route."

"Who's *they?* Who are the people that arrange for the pilots to do that?"

"It's best not to ask too many questions."

The plane arrived in the middle of a near barren desert. Surrounding a landing strip was a battalion of five companies containing one hundred soldiers each. Air Force One touched down and stopped directly in front of the centre company. Not a single soldier flinched. All remained at alert. A small observation deck wheeled up to the plane. It was so bright outside that all three Blekansits put on their sunglasses. Even Enkidu squinted somewhat from the glare. Hidden amidst the immense sunset was a camouflaged hanger with open doors. A huge canvas covered truck was the first vehicle to leave the hanger, followed by two Jeeps each with a uniquely designed gun turret. One soldier wearing a gas mask and holding a small Tupperware container walked out. She was followed by an eccentric soldier riding a unicycle while typing on a laptop computer. They arranged themselves into formation around the base of the observation deck where

Hans and his family had been joined by some high ranking officials.

"Welcome to Area 57, Mr. President," greeted General Weakbulges. "Testing ground for the most experimental and exciting weaponry in the free world. Would you care to see our top five, Sir?"

"Of course," answered Hans. "After all, they were my companies that built them. I might as well know how I'm making so much money."

"Allow me to introduce Dr. Walt Van Braun. He has been working secretly for Great Blekansit Products for over three decades."

Out of the crowd of decorated military officers walked a meek old man wearing a lab coat and carrying a clipboard. He wore glasses that were an inch thick and had tiny tuffs of white hair growing out of surprising parts of his face like his cheeks and throat. He spoke in a thick German accent.

"Yah, de weapons haf been fun to built."

"I guess that's why we pay you the big bucks," quipped Hans.

"Ju dun't pay mee. Jus keep mee hiddun from mee enemies who wish to haf me kilt."

"A great deal for both of us I'd say. Now what do you have to show me, Dr. Van Braun?"

"I might as well know how I'm making so much money."

"Vire up ze Seisma-Whoofers!" barked Van Braun.

The soldier who sat at the turrets put on some ear protectors and pressed a button to initiate the rising of two giant speakers that were attached to two giant mechanical arms. The speakers were directed towards the ground that lay directly beneath one of the companies. A low rumbling sound emitted from the contraption and grew in intensity towards its prey. The one hundred soldiers all started to vibrate. The ground beneath was shaking uncontrollably. The earth cracked in half and about forty troops fell into a gaping hole. The others were all knocked over by the various aftershocks."

"Impressive earthquake machine," commented Hans, "but do we have anything more torturous?"

"Und now ze Pyro-Psychotron!"

The soldier at the second turret stood up to a giant ray-gun and pulled its trigger. Beams of light shone towards another company of soldiers. The troops continued to stand firmly at attention.

"Nothing's happening," complained Harry.

"Yust ju vait, vittle boy," advised Van Braun.

After a few more uneventful moments, many

of the soldiers started to loosen their collars. Shortly after, many more started to scream. After a few minutes the majority of them had removed most of their clothing and were writhing on the ground in agony.

"What's happening to them?" Helena asked with concern.

"Ze ray makes dem belief dey are in vlames. Da light tricks da mind."

"Absolutely fascinating! A mind control fire ray!" exclaimed Hans. "You don't seem impressed, Helena."

"None of this has the same dignity as a good magic spell," his wife replied.

"Science is much like da magic," countered Van Braun, "yust more akkressive."

"How goes our biochemical research?" inquired Hans.

"Ve haf found avay to cultifate agressif molds dat exaggerate de most subtle repetitive aspects of man's most basic behafiours. Da most successful strain has been *randomisaproblemforus*."

Walt Van Braun nodded towards the soldier holding the container. Upon receiving her command she first checked the seal on her gas mask and proceeded to delicately open the small Tupperware container in her hands. After the lid was off she used a small hand fan to waft the contents towards an unused legion. The soldiers all began to walk uncontrollably and impulsively turn to the right. As they inevitably bumped into each other they would fall to the ground while continuing to move their legs in the same motion. They just pivoted on one of their hips, turning around and around.

"A virus that makes people run around in circles. Brilliant!" commented Hans. "Now what's in that truck?"

"Somethink a touch more tradeetional," explained Van Braun. "Release da goons!"

A latch at the back of the truck was pulled. The door flung open allowing a hoard of football players, pro-wrestlers and bar bouncers to escape like wild animals. Frothing at their mouths they proceeded to pummel one hundred soldiers to the ground.

"I had dem injected vith da rabies. It maks dem unstuppable."

"Nothing more effective than a strong fist!" Hans said gleefully. "Now do we have anything in the subtle arts? Where's my fifth column? My propaganda machine?"

"Da man vith da laptup. He influencees

almust ninety percent of da telewision, radio and internet. Tonight, must shows that da people vill vatch vill make an insult of da Danes."

The last one hundred soldiers looked at their cell phones to read various text messages stating that the Danish were evil.

"Why is he riding a unicycle?"

"He says it helps him vith da focus."

"Excellent. We'll have everyone in North America wanting a war in no time. Now how are we going to make sure that the other side will rise to the task?"

"Allow me to introduce Loki, da Trickster God of da Norse."

From behind the silent officers came a scrawny fellow with bright orange hair and a sly smile.

"Norway is right beside Denmark," explained Loki. "All I need to do is get Thor riled up and all of Scandinavia will want to fight your countries."

"Is Thor easy to sway?" asked Hans.

"He's as malleable as freshly dug up clay."

Chapter Seven

"Now class," instructed the Sacred Cow, "who can tell me the difference between *jus in bello* and *jus ad bellom*?"

Driftwood looked around and noticed that almost everyone in the room had their hands up. She hadn't even been introduced to anyone before being placed in a desk with about thirty other students.

"How were we supposed to know this?" she asked a boy beside her.

"It was part of the prescribed reading list," the boy, named Kevin, explained. "Now stop distracting me. I don't want to get in trouble."

The Sacred Cow called upon a girl in the front row.

"Jus in bello is about looking at the rules and

reasons for going to war," she clearly explained, "while Jus ad bellom studies the ethics when being in war."

"Very good. Now let's take a closer look at jus in bello or what is often referred to as the Just War Theory. When can a country go to war?"

Kevin frantically waved his arm in the air. He was anxiously grunting and squirming. The most odd thing about it was that there were at least four other students acting in a very similar fashion. The Sacred Cow finally pointed a front hoof at Kevin who inhaled a huge breath of air before he spoke.

"For a war to be considered justified, a nation must have a legitimate reason like being attacked by the other country, the declaration of war must come from the properly selected authority, the reasons for war must be morally apparent so there should be no hidden agendas and the response should be proportional to the original transgression," spoke the boy as he smiled proudly.

Another student interjected, "However, contemporary strategies allow for a first strike if it is believed that it would prevent the enemy from initiating a nuclear attack."

Driftwood was overwhelmed by the new ideas that were being quickly introduced. It was exciting and intimidating. She started to hyperventilate which was her common reaction to stressful public situations.

"Does First Strike Rationalization fit with the Just War Theory?" asked the Sacred Cow. "Discuss."

"It contradicts the idea that we must be attacked to justifiably go to war," Kevin commented.

"However, in modern times," the other student countered, "when the threat of attack is so dire as to suggest total destruction we are obligated to remove it by whatever force at our disposal."

"So if I'm taller than you," responded Kevin, "you have a right to knock me down even if I've done nothing against you but because it is possible that I may hurt you? That sounds immoral to me."

Driftwood let out a quiet yet strengthening *oomp* and a calming *ah*.

"Maybe both sides are immoral," Driftwood found herself saying aloud much to the surprise of both herself and her classmates who took notice of her for the first time.

"This seems like a good time to introduce our new student at the Regimental Conservatory," announced the Sacred Cow. "Class, this is Driftwood Ellesmere."

Driftwood waved shyly. Some of the students smiled back at her while others whispered to each other.

"Isn't she kind of famous?"

"I hear she knows a lot about magic already."

"I hear she didn't have to take the entrance exam."

"That's not fair. And what do you think about her hair?"

"Please. The simple straight look is so thirty years ago."

The comments soon subsided as everyone continued to stare at Driftwood. The boy beside her sought clarification.

"What did you mean by both sides being immoral?"

"How can someone ever justify war?" asked Driftwood.

"But what if you're attacked?"

"Maybe punching back is the traditional response but it may be just an archaic and immature idea. It's what little kids do. Perhaps we as a society could find a better way to work with an opponent."

"Have you ever heard of Ghandi?" the Sacred Cow asked.

"I think so," Driftwood replied. "Wasn't he a bald guy who wore a bed sheet?"

"He lived simply in India which is where I am from. For hundreds of years the British had ruled over the people of India even though Britain was in another part of the world. Inspired by Henry David Thoreau, an American writer, Ghandi led one of the first *non-violent revolutions*. Ghandi wore a basic robe to protest the British textile industry. He led thousands of people to the sea to gather their own salt so that they didn't depend on the British monopoly over that substance. Soon the people of India refused to follow any British orders. The British soldiers would strike them down and the citizens offered no aggressive response. The British could not maintain their rule without publicly beating down the residents of India. The strategy was difficult as it took great discipline to be beaten and do nothing. However, the British soon realized the fallacy of their rule and eventually allowed India to pursue independence. It is one of the most unique mass movements in history as it was almost entirely passive. And it all occurred because someone asked if there was another way to do things. Much like what Driftwood just did."

Driftwood was starting to see benefits in school.

Chapter Eight

RECRUIT

"You've done what?" Chuck Wood asked in disbelief.

"I've joined the army," repeated Del Wood to his father. "It seems like the only way to get out of Emporia and see the world. I'm taking a bus to the base this afternoon."

"Why didn't you talk to me? I could have helped you travel."

"Dad, the hardware store has barely done any business since the Blekan-Mart opened up and I never want to go and work for them again. This way you won't have to worry about me. I'll even be able to send you money from my military paycheque."

"I didn't want this for you, Del."

"It's not about what you want. It's about the

army needing me. The Danish could attack us at any moment."

"Who told you that?"

"An army recruiter at the mall. He said that a Danish terrorist had bombed a Blekan-Mart in Kansas City last week."

"That's ridiculous!"

The tense discussion was interrupted by Anne Wood, Chuck's mother, who ran into the living room with a cordless phone in one hand and a drippy eggbeater in the other.

"Great news," she announced. "I just got off the phone with Old Bart who called from Ellesmere Island to say that Driftwood has returned. She had been off on another planet for the last year."

Anne Wood was Driftwood's grandmother, Chuck was her uncle and Del was her cousin. The other member of the Wood household was Rotten Wood, Driftwood's grandfather. Her mother, Eva Wood, had married Hans Blekansit only to flee from him while pregnant because Hans had hit her. The main reason why she did not return home to instead journey to Ellesmere Island was because Rotten Wood had frequently beaten Eva and her brother, Chuck, when they were growing up. Subsequently,

Driftwood wasn't reunited with her family until recently when Old Bart, her longtime guardian, had reconnected them. Unloved and ignored in his own home, Rotten Wood had wasted the last twenty years sitting in his easy chair watching television. Anne Wood did not even bother to tell her husband that their grand-daughter wasn't dead as suspected. While she still cooked him meals with devotion they had basically stopped communicating beyond her brief pleasantries and his despondent grunts.

Anne, Chuck and Del celebrated while Anne explained how Driftwood was already on some other adventure and had no time for a visit. Rotten Wood found the jubilant noises in the room next to him distracting as he tried to focus on a game show. He used his cane to shut the door. His efforts were unnecessary as Del's decision to join the army quelled the excitement. Del was soon saying a tearful goodbye to his grandmother. Chuck drove his son to the bus station. Anne continued to bake cookies.

Rotten was able to re-engage in his game show. However, as he focused mindlessly on the spinning wheel, his view of the screen was unexpectedly blocked by the spectral image of a woman's head. Rotten Wood clutched at his chest. A full ghost emerged and floated above him.

"Hey howdy, Dad, did you miss me these last twenty years?"

Eva Wood knew how to make an entrance.

Chapter Nine

NORWEGIAN POLITIYOYO

The Norse Myths have a story about the end of the world. Ragnarök was the word they had for the end of days. It meant 'the doom of the gods'. However, some ancient texts call the event, Ragnarökk, the extra letter changing the translation to mean 'the twilight of the gods'. Like a sunset, 'twilight' does signify decline and a closing of a period. However, it allows for rebirth in a way that 'doom' seems to dismiss.

Being older than both words, Freya used to never concern herself with the distinction. She had seen a few apocalypses over the eons. While her own return helped reinforce the Ragnarökk spelling, each ending had brought about enough bloody pointless violence to remind her of the accuracy of Ragnarök and its connotations of calamity.

To her, death was inevitable for all mortal things. However, she had been hoping to help the planet have better Ragnarökks; to make bedtime a little sweeter and have things come to a close more like a fairytale than a horror story. Inspired by Driftwood's efforts to save the world, Freya was joined by her fellow Valkarie who consciously re-entered the world to actively engage in its development. In the last year, Freya had become elected leader of the Socialist Left Party in the parliament of Norway. Her party was dedicated to finding government solutions that helped all citizens. The Centre Party had the most elected representatives so their leader was prime minister. The Socialist Left Party had enough seats to give the Centre Party a majority if they sided together so Freya had influence over the prime minister's actions. She had been encouraging him to take a peaceful stance in the growing conflict between Denmark and Canada. However, recent developments had threatened the precarious balance of power. Three of the Centre Party's representatives had to resign due to various scandals. If the Labour Party won those seats they would takeover having the most seats in the house. As well, they could combine with the Progress Party to gain majority power. All the parties were normally very liberal minded and promoted peace, however, the Labour Party was also electing a new leader today. That new leader could dictate a new political direction for Norway. The by-election's results were soon to be announced.

Freya begrudgingly studied some circle graphs while she waited in her office for the results. It felt like she spent more time with statistics than with people. Looking at numbers while waiting for other numbers. It was at moments like this that she missed her flying chariot and battleaxe. Her contemplation was interrupted by her assistant.

"The results are on television now, Madame Leader."

Freya turned on the news. She was shocked to see Odin, Loki and Thor all standing at a podium. When she recently saw Odin in the Land of Crawling Light, he was off to rejoin his sons in an international hunt for Blekan-Mart vomiting giants. The last time they were in Norway they were conducting illegal whaling. Freya was gravely concerned to see their surprise return. The scrolling news banner at the bottom of the screen explained that the three gods had returned yesterday to be surprise write-in candidates for the Labour Party. They had won all three of the open seats and now, in coalition with the Progess Party, had majority power in the assembly of elected representatives. It was also revealed that through a hasty and irregular selection process, Odin was now leader of his party. He had become Prime Minister of Norway less than a day after his return.

"We shall reclaim our title as the greatest warriors of the world and assist Denmark with any conflict they may have with Canada and its allies," Odin announced in his acceptance speech.

"Oh you stupid, stupid Viking," she sighed. "Why couldn't you have just given peace a chance?"

Chapter Ten

MORE IS LESSON

Dear Driftwood,

I hope this letter gets to you. Murph said that he would make sure it was delivered although he wouldn't tell us where your school is. I bet you're learning lots to save the world.

Things at camp are pretty fun but we sure do miss you. Glacier, Lichen, Stormy and I have started a band. We rehearse after the campers go to sleep. I'm playing bass. We asked Rose to join us but she's getting pretty caught up with researching current events.

Take care,
Tide
xoxo

Driftwood's heart jumped every time she read the *xoxo* under Tide's name. Tide had asked Driftwood out just before Peter Z. Juice brought her to the Regimental Conservatory. She put the letter away for fear that it would be confiscated by her teacher.

Michael Magee walked softly amongst the desk rows, telling one of the oldest stories ever while students ranged in degrees of attention. Some took notes. Some scribbled half-abstract, half-realistic images. Others daydreamed. Driftwood preferred to listen to the story without taking notes.

"Thousands of years ago, the city of Urak had a great king called Gilgamesh," he began.

This one statement was enough to inspire a few students to whisper to each other. Peter Z. Juice had a ghostly servant with the same name. It was anticipated that the strange spectre's origins were about to be shared. Even the doodlers started to pay better attention.

"However, Gilgamesh was very unhappy and subsequently, was a very cruel king," continued Michael Magee. "The main problem was that he was lonely. As everyone worshipped him there was no one to be his friend. And so the people of the land prayed to the gods for a peer to be created. Using moist clay, the goddess Aruru shaped and fashioned a being. She created Enkidu, a beast man who ran wild in the forest. Due to his rough and untamed mania, no humans could safely approach Enkidu until the love of a priestess named Shamhat calmed the man enough to enter society. When Enkidu and Gilgamesh first met in Urak they fought intensely. Yet by virtue of their equal skill, they became great friends in the process. Enkidu tempered Gilgamesh, who rose to become a great and benevolent ruler. As well, Enkidu joined Gilgamesh on many adventures, including the defeat of Humbaba, guardian of the Cedar Forest."

"Wait a second," interrupted Driftwood. "These guys defeated someone who protects a forest and they're considered heroes?"

"Your observation," returned Michael, "although rudely interruptive, is fair. However, it was a different time. We can also view their exploits as a symbol of humanity's early reliance on wood as a material for progress. Now, please let me continue.

"After the duos successful pillaging of the Cedar Forest, Gilgamesh was romantically approached by the goddess, Ishtar. Gilgamesh spurned her advances provoking Ishtar to summon the Bull of Heaven to battle in her honour. Gilgamesh and Enkidu defeated the Bull, however not without raising the ire of the eternals. The gods decided that in response to the killing of the forest sentinel Hambaba and the Bull of Heaven, that one of the two adventurers must die. They inflicted a fatal disease upon Enkidu. After Enkidu's tragic demise, Gilgamesh's life began to unravel and he soon became unshaven, unclean and trapped in an extreme depression. He finally mustered up some courage and decided to seek immortality. After near certain failure, a god gave him a plant that is said to grant one eternal life. In a cowardly move he decided to take the leaves back to Urak to test on someone before trying them himself. However, when he was asleep at his campsite a snake slithered up and stole his plant, thus ending Gilgamesh's quest for endlessness."

A well-timed bell signified that class was over. Driftwood wasn't used to everyone getting up so automatically. The way they grabbed their books and rose in unison at each ringing sound, the other students looked to her like robots.

"What kind of a magic school is this?"

Driftwood asked Kevin. "We haven't practiced a single spell."

"The Regimental Conservatory believes in laying a strong foundation of philosophy and history," he explained. "However, we'll get to work on precognitions in the next class."

Driftwood followed Kevin into a room that had no desks which she found quite a relief. The students all sat in a circle around their teacher, the Seer of Eternal Beyonds. Driftwood still found it strange that the Seer was a rock. To the right of the static stone was Simia, the Seer's gorilla transporter. To the left was Illumina, the Seer's translator and a being of light. Illumina began to speak.

"Today we shall meditate to achieve a state of pure immobile tranquility. It is in this state that visions of the future can often appear. However, do not be tricked as your own mind might create false prophecies. Now breathe in with an *ah* and an *oomp*."

"Excuse me," interrupted Driftwood, "but I was taught to breathe out my *oomps* and *ahs*."

After a few moments of consultation with the Seer, Illumina responded.

"Sometimes we must unlearn things to gain new insights. Now do what has been instructed."

Driftwood tried her best to reverse her long practice methods but found it hard to ignore her muscle memory.

"I can't do it," she gagged. "It's giving me the hiccups."

Driftwood looked around and noticed that all the other students were breathing in oomps and ahs without any trouble. She closed her eyes and tried again. Although she struggled at the start, Driftwood soon found herself in the appropriate rhythm.

"Now I want you to lose yourself in time," the Seer explained via Illumina. "Ignore the moment. Expand your perspective to the infinite. As you gaze at the darkness of your eyelids find an area that is a lighter shade of black. Let that lightness expand into vision. Allow the future to open up to you."

"Yiiii!" screamed Driftwood loud enough that most of the other students were disrupted from seeing their visions. Many of them grumbled in annoyance.

"What happened?" asked Kevin.

"I saw a nuclear bomb launching," explained Driftwood.

"You probably were just seeing an image that was conjured by your subconscious. Many people our age harbor fears of atomic war. I doubt it was a future vision. Prophecies at our stage are usually personal and nuclear bombs are far from personal."

"They kind of are when your father is the President of the United States."

Chapter Eleven

DECLARATION CONTEMPLATION

The delegates of the NATO member nations apprehensively watched a giant television screen as Hans Blekansit made a public address. Clover and the other pages were standing at the back of the assembly hall.

"My fellow Americans, it has come to my attention that a Danish geologist has stepped her foot onto the rocky shore of Hans Island," the President of the United States announced. "We have encouraged Canada to view this as an act of aggression. Subsequently, Canada and the United States have declared war on Denmark. We will be assured victory because, even as we speak, the best weaponry that Great Blekansit Products has to offer is being shipped to the Arctic. Thank you and good night."

When the television screen turned off, the first person to do anything was the delegate from Denmark, Hamlet Jørgensen, who threw a stapler at Donald Mackenzie, the Canadian delegate. Mackenzie ran towards Jørgensen and attempted to body check him but was blocked by the Norwegian delegate. The American delegate tossed a hole puncher at the Norwegian delegate. The rest of the delegates were cheering for the various sides. The Dutch Secretary General sadly shook his head. He knew that this declaration of war was causing a fracture in NATO that may never be repaired. One of the oldest organizations in the world dedicated to peace and security had been reduced to a chorus of infighting.

Clover snuck out the back door of the assembly hall. She sought out the closest exit as she desperately needed some fresh air. Finding a patch of grass near the NATO Headquarters, Clover laid down, stretched out her limbs and looked at the sky. She turned her head and noticed that a dove had landed beside her.

"Hello, little birdy," Clover greeted in a whistle-like voice. "If I was like my friend Driftwood you would be able to understand me."

The dove pecked at the ground.

"I think it'd be nice to be a bird," Clover continued. "It seems like animals have a better sense of peace and tranquility than us humans."

The dove poked at its wing.

"Little birdy, I wish that you could help us," contemplated Clover, "be more like you."

The dove flew away. A cloud was breaking up and slowly letting sunlight shine through. Clover tried to let the warm rays comfort her. The dove returned and landed on Clover's outstretched arm. It was soon joined by another dove that perched itself on Clover's leg. A third dove joined them, followed by more until Clover had almost a hundred birds atop her. With their talons gently clenching Clover's clothing the doves started to fly away carrying the young girl with them. Clover had seen enough strange events with Driftwood that she easily surrendered to the doves' bizarre behaviour and let them carry her away. The flock began to fly north anticipating Clover's wishes.

"Take me away, little birdies, to the heart of this worldly conflict."

Chapter Twelve

A HISTORY OF ABUSE

"What's the matter, Dad? Never seen a ghost before? Surprised that your estranged daughter has returned after all these years?"

Eva Wood floated circles around a rapid breathing Rotten Wood. The old man's eyes opened wider than they had in years. His hands firmly gripped the sides of his armchair. His tensed fingers moved up the upholstery until he had two fists made.

Years ago, Eva's father was known as Cotton Wood. He was a well respected carpenter in Emporia, Kansas. The town council enlisted him to rebuild the bridge that ran over the Cottonwood River. Cotton took great pride in constructing the bridge that ran over his namesake river. However, he used wood that was unknowingly contaminated with termites. The bridge soon collapsed. Cotton Wood quickly became viewed as an unreliable carpenter. Some people started to cruelly call him Rotten Wood which stuck in the community. The name and the shame changed him. As his pride in his work dissipated, his self worth equally decayed. He became an angry man. This fury lasted throughout his marriage. He used to take his rage out on his two children. Eva ran away from home. Chuck eventually was able to stand up to his father. Rotten Wood had spent the last decade doing very little, stewing in the juices of a life isolated by violent choices.

"I came back to say that you were a horrible father!" cried Eva. "You beat me and Chuck. We always blamed ourselves for every blow you struck. I ran away from home and joined that TV show *Fight for Love* to escape you. You scared me into the arms of a cruel husband. I died trying to find my daughter a safe home. I never got to see Mom or Chuck again."

Eva was not really certain why she decided to haunt her father. She just couldn't let him get away without ever knowing how she felt. She felt an impulse to take advantage of her ghostly form to confront those who had wronged her in the past. However, she had not thought through how her father may respond.

A fist flew through Eva's head. She let out a scream of memory as Rotten punched a lamp into pieces. He swung again, not yet realizing that his daughter had no physicality to make contact with, and lost his balance, falling into the television set. As it crashed to the ground the screen cracked in seven spots. Eva disappeared into the ground, traumatized by the sight of her rampaging father. Anne Wood came in to see what the unusual commotion was about.

Anne Wood was born Anne deMage. Her mother, Christine deMage, had raised Anne by herself. In those days, single mothers were often socially ostracized. Anne, while raised lovingly by Christine, was shy and did not meet people easily. When she met Rotten Wood she was attracted to his bad reputation. She and her mother had been frequently scoffed at so she could relate to Rotten. In his more youthful days, Rotten was able to present his anger with a bit of swagger. Her love tended to temper him and he never laid a hand on her. Her love for him also blinded her to the fact that he hit their children. She

"What's the matter, Dad?"

had repressed the idea of abuse for so long that the notion of it was inconceivable.

Rotten had just released what was an unfortunately large amount of pent up hostility. Anne watched as Rotten thrashed about the den.

"Oh Rotten, my dear," she pleaded, "please calm down."

Her husband was untamable, unstoppable. His wrath consumed him. After smashing every family portrait that hung on the walls he swung at his wife for the first time in their decades-long marriage.

The impact of the punch sent Anne sailing out of the room. Gasping and weeping she crawled back into the kitchen and reached for the telephone. She was in so much shock that she mindlessly pressed buttons on the receiver. The first button she pressed was for the callback function. The phone dialed up the last person who had called.

Old Bart was sitting on the porch of Ellesmere Island's Toque and Mitt Inn, watching an ice wall collapse into the Arctic waters due to global warming, when he heard the phone ring.

Chapter Thirteen

READY ... SET ... ACTIVISM!

"I'm telling you guys there are more important things than music right now," stammered Rose.

Tide, Glacier, Stormy and Lichen were tuning their instruments and getting ready to rehearse when Rose barged into Camp Magee's staff cabin. Glacier and Lichen both strummed guitars. Stormy banged his drums and Tide played his bass guitar.

"Go easy, Rose," defended Glacier. "We've spent the whole day working with kids."

"We have fun doing this," added Lichen.

"Maybe we'll even get a gig soon," said Tide.

"Perhaps we should listen to what Rose has to say," countered Stormy.

"Canada has declared war on Denmark," announced Rose.

"We know," said Glacier. "You told us this morning and yesterday and the day before that."

"We have to do something!"

"But what can we do?" asked Lichen. "We're a bunch of camp counselors on the west coast."

"I talked to Swamp," explained Rose. "There are no campers coming next week. He was planning on having us do maintenance around the site but was supportive if we wanted to go and join the protest."

"What protest?" asked Stormy.

"People are gathering outside of the Parliament Building in Ottawa," explained Rose. "They are trying to let the politicians and the public know that many people are against the war."

"Ottawa?" repeated Tide. "But that's in Ontario"

"So what?"

"It's thousands of kilometres away."

"Murph told me that he would use money from his gold to fly us there if we wanted."

There was a silence as everyone contemplated their new opportunity.

Rose is right, thought Lichen.

What would Driftwood do? Tide asked himself, knowing the answer.

It could be fun, contemplated Glacier.

I'll have to report this to my superiors, Stormy thought, *and await further instructions.*

"Let's do it!" they all yelled in apparent agreement.

Chapter Fourteen

THE PROBLEM WITH STRICT

"Come on, Edie" Driftwood enthusiastically encouraged. "You can do it! Flap as hard as you can!"

Driftwood and Edie were in the gymnasium of the Regimental Conservatory enjoying a rare moment of free time. Driftwood was mounted atop Edie as the eaderion was trying desperately to fly with a passenger. Edie stumbled on her eight legs until she finally started to dig her claws into the gym floor. With sturdier balance she gained significant momentum. She soon lifted off the ground and soared with the grace of an eagle.

"Yahoo!" bellowed Driftwood as the two of them did three loops in mid-air. "I knew you could do it!"

The joyous flight was disturbed by the ringing of the school bell. Break-time was over. Edie tried to land majestically but instead the two tumbled and somersaulted overtop each other.

"Ka-roar!" the Eaderion purred. "Edie fly high!"

"You bet you did, buddy," complimented Driftwood, petting Edie affectionately as she stood up and made her way to class.

Driftwood sat beside Kevin in the computer lab.

"I hate this class the most," complained Driftwood.

"The Grand Cubile does a great job of teaching magically enhanced technology," responded Kevin as he snapped his fingers. An image of Kevin and Driftwood dancing at a disco suddenly appeared on his computer screen. "We can create anything we want."

"Yuck. Just another example of how technology fulfills false fantasies."

Kevin was hurt by the response.

"Why are you here if you don't want to learn what the Regimental Conservatory teaches?"

"Good question. I didn't ask to come to this school. I think I should be dealing with my father. Now can you please get that image of us dancing off your screen?"

Kevin snapped his fingers again and an internet news site popped up on the monitor. Driftwood glanced at the headline. Her jaw dropped.

WAR DECLARED BY
PRESIDENT BLEKANSIT

Before Driftwood had even really processed the news, the Grand Cubile floated into the room. The hive of populated honeycombs hovered amidst the pods of computer learning stations.

"Clazz," it buzzed, "today we will learn about divining ze perfect webzite."

"Is that headline real or fake?" Driftwood questioned Kevin.

"Who iz talking?"

"Come on, Kevin. Why do you always pretend like you don't know me during lessons?"

A bee flew out of the floating hive and stung Driftwood on the back of the neck.

"Ouch!" she screamed.

"Lazt warning," the Grand Cubile

commanded. "No zpeaking out of turn."

"You stung me!"

"You were being dizciplined."

"I'll show you discipline."

Driftwood waved her hand and made a calm incantation.

"Bees Sneeze," she chanted.

It is a very rare but volatile thing for a bee to sneeze. When hundreds of them all sneeze at the same time inside a bee hive it can cause quite a disturbance to their equilibrium. Dealing with the impact of many bees ricocheting off its honeycomb walls, the Grand Cubile began to wobble and twirl. Many of the students found themselves laughing at their teacher's expense.

"You zhall be ezcorted away immediately!" declared the Grand Cubile.

Driftwood was soon being led down a hallway by Gilgamesh, the ghostly servant. Driftwood recalled the story she was told in history class.

"Didn't you used to be a king?" she found herself asking the tall, tired spirit.

"That was a long time ago," explained Gilgamesh, "when I was vigorously alive. I had many adventures back then. Now, I must bide my time until I regain more physicality."

"I've also had a few adventures," boasted Driftwood, "although they often get me into a fair amount of trouble."

"For myself as well. My clumsy decisions ultimately left me alone for my dying days."

"Don't be too bummed out. It's thousands of years later and your story is still being told."

"It often feels like a punishment to have one's feats of failure immortalized and celebrated."

"Maybe it's the things that make us weak that capture the similarities we all relate to," contemplated Driftwood. "Misery loves company and that kind of thing. However, we also get inspiration from stories that illustrate success. The combination is what makes for the dramas and comedies of our collective histories. Clara, one of the people who raised me, used to say that. She's an Inuit shaman who taught me how to look at stories as messages from an older, deeper existence."

"I never had a teacher, only a best friend named Enkidu," lamented Gilgamesh.

"I heard things didn't end well with you guys," said Driftwood.

"I endangered his life numerous times until death finally took his soul."

"Maybe he's come back like you have."

"Nonsense! It has taken me thousands of years to return and only the dense gravity of Jupiter's core allows me to have any notion of a physical form. I doubt Enkidu could have been as resourceful and strong-willed as I was. He was never my equal."

The two arrived outside the office of Peter Z. Juice. Gilgamesh tried unsuccessfully to open the door but failed every time as his hand would pass right through the door handle.

"Would you like a hand with that?" Driftwood asked.

"Please," Gilgamesh meekly replied. "He wants to see you alone anyways."

"Did you know that the term public school has two entirely different meanings depending on what part of the world you are in? In Canada and the United States the term public school means a school supported by the taxes of its citizens with the intention of providing every child in its country with an education. In the United Kingdom, Australia and many other Commonwealth countries a public school is privately owned and the family of the pupil must pay significant fees. What the US calls a public school is known as a state school in the UK. Amazing how words change meaning depending on where you are."

After accumulating some debating experience in her various classes, Driftwood had grown less intimidated by Peter Z. Juice's spontaneous lectures.

"I know about the various school systems," replied Driftwood. "I read about them in the Encyclopedia Worldattica volumes that I studied while I grew up at the Toque and Mitt Inn. It doesn't matter what you call it, something slightly stinks about your pedagogy."

"Pardon me? As a society we strive to empower every student to attain the highest peak of knowledge as passed down from generation to generation. The Regimental Conservatory is a shining example of providing a comprehensive education in academics and magic."

"I don't doubt that. But I have a question for you. How did the other students get in here?"

"They are selected through a rigourous and competitive selection process. However, all acceptable candidates are granted free tuition. The Order is highly supportive of providing instruction to students of great potential."

"Do the other students know that they are in a school that is under an ocean of liquid hydrogen on the surface of Jupiter's core and protected only by a giant clear dome?"

"After three years of attendance in our program we reveal that fact to them. The young ones and most new initiates think we are in the Swiss Alps."

"Most new initiates?"

"You were an exception."

"What exactly am I being initiated into?"

"The Order of the Good and True, of course."

"I don't recall signing up for anything."

"Pardon me?"

"I mean I came with you because you told me that I needed to help you save the world. Instead, I've been talked at endlessly, scolded regularly and even stung by a bee."

"Did you know that bee stings are a symbol of-"

"Let me stop you right there, Mr. Juice," Driftwood interrupted. "It's my turn for a lecture. Did you know that most countries consider a residential school the same thing as a boarding school where the students live on campus? However, in Canada the term residential school has a specific and grave meaning. Beginning before the nineteenth century, the Canadian government and church missionaries took young native children from their families and tribes and forced them to live in boarding schools where they would learn how to speak English and be taught other components of European culture. While seemingly noble in intent, as who can argue with a quality education, the residential schools have been exposed over time as horrible places of abuse and mistreatment. As well, an analysis of their intentions can easily show that the Canadian government had no respect for the cultures that existed on this continent before the Europeans settled here. Some have said that it was one of the many examples where one culture attempts to destroy another culture. A genocide of ideas and beliefs. After over a hundred years the Canadian government has finally apologized for their behaviour. Can you see where I'm going with this, Mr. Juice?"

"I am familiar with Canada's residential schooling crisis," responded Peter Z. Juice, "but I am having difficulty following your reasoning for bringing it up."

"It all leads to me saying *I quit.*"

"You can't do that."

"I just did. Now can you please get me back to Earth? It's time to confront my father."

Chapter Fifteen

FLYING HEROES ON ICE

Hermit the Laughing Man, AKA Heinz Blekansit, AKA the father of Hans Blekansit, AKA the grandfather of both Harry Blekansit and Driftwood Ellesmere, was visiting Old Bart at the Toque and Mitt Inn. Heinz was hoping to get Old Bart and Murph Magee to reassemble as giant fighters now that all three had almost completely healed their bones that were broken from being collectively stepped on by a very large foot. He had been sitting on the deck of the hotel when Old Bart had gone inside to answer the phone. He decided to occupy his mind by stroking his long beard while writing short lines of poetry.

With dark so long
And ice so white
Vision so strong
Arctic's pure sight

His meditative rhyming was interrupted when Old Bart ran out onto the deck in a frantic state.

"Hermit, we need to get to Kansas quick!" he exclaimed. "Driftwood's grandmother is in trouble."

"Driftwood's grandmother? Has she returned from the dead?" asked Heinz in dismay, thinking that Old Bart was referring to Stephanie Blekansit, his wife who had been killed by their son Hans Blekansit.

"From the other side of her family," Old Bart explained. "Eva Wood's mother. Do you have a method to get us to Emporia quickly?"

The Laughing Man waved his hands at a chunk of ice that floated in the nearby bay. He continued his chant.

It's colder not hotter
Yet ice floats on water
Now may it also dare
To rise fast through air

The slab of frozen water elevated itself out of the ocean and hovered beside the two men, allowing them to step aboard. Within seconds they were soaring through the sky at breakneck speed.

Rotten Wood smacked the phone out of Anne Wood's hands shortly after she had began fumbling with it. She evaded his grasp and ran through the other kitchen door into the dining room. Rotten followed her and in his rage smashed into the hutch that held generations-old china that was instantly shattered into numerous pieces. Anne took advantage of his clumsiness and escaped into the living room. Rotten was soon after her again. She desperately threw some couch pillows at him but he easily swatted them away. However, it granted her enough time to race into their entranceway and out the front door. The sudden daylight blinded Anne and she tripped over a bush in their yard. Before she could get up her hair was gripped by Rotten Wood's strong hands. He pulled her up, causing her great pain.

"Please, Rotten, don't you realize what you're doing?"

"Raaargh!"

*Within seconds they were soaring
through the sky at breakneck speed.*

A screaming man
A kindly lady
Two guys on ice
Now ain't this crazy

Anne Wood looked up to see two elderly men soaring down from the sky on a small block of ice. One of the men was spouting poetry. The other was scratching his nose. The sky was quickly darkening with storm clouds.

"Leave your wife alone," commanded Old Bart, "or face our mighty power."

Rotten ignored the ultimatum raised his fist and began to swing. Hermit's long beard stretched out as if it was a living tentacle and grabbed Anne Wood's wrist. As the hair curled up she was pulled out of harm's way.

"Watchoo!" sneezed Old Bart, cueing a lightning bolt to strike Rotten Wood on the spot.

The violent man collapsed on the ground in smoldering shock.

Chapter Sixteen

DIFFERENT PERSPECTIVES

"Dad, come quick!" yelled Harry from the drawing room of the White House residency.

"What is it?" Hans shouted back.

"The battle's beginning!"

"About time," muttered Hans.

Harry, Helena and Enkidu the electrical being were watching cable news on a big screen television. Hans ran out of the bathroom as a toilet flushed behind him. The first image that he saw was of American and Canadian soldiers firing their guns over a wall of sandbags. The camera slowly panned over the sandbags and showed Danish and Norwegian soldiers being shot.

"This is awesome!" exclaimed Harry. "It's better than a video game."

"Show some restraint, Harry," Helena advised. "Bloodlust is quite unappealing."

The television screen was suddenly filled with an image of Thor, the Norse thunder god, flying towards the American and Canadian trench and smashing the bags with his hammer. The soldiers went flying everywhere, giving the Danish and Norwegian troops an edge in the combat. Hans picked up the nearest telephone.

"Send in the Area 57 weaponry," he commanded, "and get something to the Canadians to help them with the peaceniks who are causing such a ruckus. Time to flex our muscle."

Before he had time to hang up the phone the windows of the drawing room suddenly shattered. In moments Secret Service Agents rushed in to protect the First Family.

"Not again," complained Hans. "What sort of security does the White House have? You guys always come in after the glass is broken."

Edie the Eaderion hovered outside the window, carrying with her a lone passenger.

"Don't blame them, Father," advised Driftwood. "I can be quite stealthy when I want to be."

The Secret Service immediately fired their

"The battle's beginning!"

pistols at the invaders.

"Cotton balls," incanted Driftwood with a wave of her hand.

Tiny harmless wads of raw thread bounced off both girl and beast.

"So, Daughter, you grace us with your presence at last," greeted Hans. "I was thinking you had forgotten about my side of your family."

"It's a side I often hope to forget but you're quite difficult to ignore. I hear you've started a pointless international war."

Edie flew through the window. Her attempt to land was unsuccessful and the duo tumbled chaotically, eventually knocking over the giant television. A crack spread throughout its screen.

"Thank you, Driftwood," Hans said. "Taxpayers pay to replace that television and, because it's a Great Blekansit Product, the money goes to me. Which happens also to be the point of the war."

"Point?" huffed Driftwood, that crash having knocked the wind out of her.

The guards were all lunging forward to restrain the threat.

"Geckos," cast Driftwood regaining herself.

Seven Secret Service agents transformed into small lizards wearing black ties and sunglasses.

"What is the point of countries that have been allies for over a century suddenly sending soldiers to try and kill each other?" Driftwood inquired.

"Money," Hans replied succinctly.

"Why am I not surprised?"

"Peace is not profitable if a large portion of your company is involved in weapons development. I needed war. Why did you think I became President of the United States? It was the easiest way to insure a world of conflict for at least four years."

"How did you get Canada and Denmark to involve themselves in your profiteering?"

"Oh, the Canada-Denmark squabble over Hans Island has been going on for years. The Arctic may seem desolate but many countries have interest in its geographical distribution. As global warming melts the ice up there, a small rock like Hans Island could be instrumental in a future northwest passage of travel. And trust me, at the rate that oil is being consumed, air travel will soon be a very rare thing. Boats will be the new planes. Which leads well into the other reason wee Hans Island is sought after. The Arctic may be one of the last places on Earth left with reachable oil. Every extra square foot claimed by a country could mean privileged access to the last drops of a highly sought-after resource."

"Sounds like greed and self-interest run high in international circles."

"You have no idea, Daughter, and I've just been a very good player."

"The word good belongs nowhere near you, Father, so, while informative, this conversation is now over. I can't let you go on with this."

Driftwood began to wave and cast. Before she finished outstretching her arm she was assaulted by a stream of electricity emitting from Enkidu's hands.

"Aargh!" Driftwood screamed.

Edie swooped forward and swiped her front paws at the electrical being. Enkidu aimed one of his hands at the Eaderion and blasted the creature against the ceiling, while his other hand continued to flood Driftwood with painful energy.

"Excellent work, Enkidu," commented Hans. "Don't be afraid to fry them to a crisp."

Driftwood writhed on the floor while Edie was pinned to the ceiling with Enkidu blasting endlessly at both of them. Harry watched with glee as his half-sister was being tortured. Helena, however, was looking sad as she raised her fingers towards Enkidu. She flicked her wrist. Enkidu felt a wall of force push against him. Falling over he stopped his discharge of energies, giving relief to both Driftwood and Edie.

"What are you doing?" a flabbergasted Hans asked his wife.

"Something very important," Helena replied as she walked over and wrapped her arms around Driftwood. "Enough with this guise. Time for me to go to work."

A spiral of light wrapped around the two ladies. They disappeared as the light shot out the broken window.

"What's up with Mom?" asked Harry.

"It looks like she wasn't the faithful wife and mother she made herself out to be," deduced Hans. "I suspected as much. Let's look at the bright side of all this, Son."

"What's that?"

"We have an Eaderion in our possession again and they're always good for business."

Chapter Seventeen

ALL WE ARE SAYING

Thousands of people were gathered on the steps of the Canada's Parliament Building. Armed with signs and slogans they hoped to send a message to Ottawa that something was rotten with the Denmark conflict. Police officers wearing helmets and carrying shields surrounded the crowd, their dark uniforms in stark contrast to the rainbow-coloured outfits of the protesters.

"What do we want?" yelled a rally organizer into her megaphone.

"Peace!" responded the crowd.

"When do we want it?"

"Now!"

This is fun, thought Glacier.

Doing this is right, Lichen affirmed to herself.

Driftwood would be impressed, felt Tide.

I'm so grateful that everyone came, realized Rose.

The kids are alright, contemplated Murph Magee.

Now's the time to act, Stormy prompted himself.

Stormy approached a couple of young men who appeared more restless and angry than the other attendants of the rally.

"Hey, guys," he began, "don't those police officers annoy the heck out of you?"

"What do you mean?" asked one of them.

"We come out here to have a peaceful rally and they show up to intimidate us," Stormy continued.

"What should we do about it?" asked the other.

"Show them that we don't need them here," Stormy said as he handed rocks to both of them. "The only way we're going to have peace is to fight for it."

"What should we do with these?" the first guy asked.

"What do you think?" replied Stormy. "Throw them at the cops."

In unison, the two guys hurled their stones

at the police officers. One rock hit a shield and the other smacked into a helmet. No one was hurt but it prompted the line of officers to push forward onto the crowd. Within moments, dozens of protesters were knocked to the ground. Some of the other activists were upset by the police interference and pushed back towards the shields. The police started to club people with batons. More citizens began to hurtle debris at the officers. Without receiving any orders from his superiors, one policeman nervously rapidly fired rubber bullets at the crowd. Rose was struck on the shoulder.

"Holey Ma-Joley!" she cried. "Things are getting out of hand. What happened?"

"I hate to say it," said Lichen as she comforted Rose's wound, "but I think I know how this started."

"How?"

"Stormy may be an agent provocateur."

Chapter Eighteen

A FLOWER IN YOUR HAIR

A drum circle was ripping it up on the slopes of Golden Gate Park's Hippie Hill near the edge of the Haight-Ashbury community in San Francisco. Three girls in tie dye dresses were dancing about. A juggler was twirling flaming devil sticks. Folks were kicking a hacky sack. Only if they were coincidentally looking up at a specific moment would the people in the park have been able to see a bolt of light arch across the sky and twist around itself below the street post that held both the Haight Street and Ashbury Street signs to produce two hugging women out of thin air.

"The last time you did that to me you teleported me into a tree!" chastised Driftwood as she pushed Helena away. "I had to become nothing to escape exploding from over-densification."

"Which was a good way to teach you how to manifest survival value from existential thought," responded Helena. "If my sources are correct, you ended up meeting your mother's ghost on that little adventure."

"Is any part of my life private?"

"Not likely. Anyhow, Driftwood, would you believe me if I told you that I was an agent for a group that you will take great interest in meeting?"

"If it's the Order of the Good and True then the answer is no thanks."

"Oh I guarantee that it is something and somewhere completely different. They are a little less rigid in their structure and don't seek to control anything."

"Sounds intriguing. Let's go then."

"We can't."

"What? You make a big deal about this group and then say we can't go meet them?"

"Well, you can't yet. I have to teach you how to prepare yourself for travel to their realm."

"I'm kind of tired of teachers."

"Then imagine I'm an encyclopedia or a computer search engine or whatnot and pretend that you're learning independently. To proceed, you must first figure out how to complete yourself."

"Pardon me? Do what to myself?"

"Complete yourself. Become balanced with your inner being."

"What do you mean by that?"

"Embrace this paradox – the only way I can complete myself is to realize that I will never be complete."

The two stood silently for a fairly extended period of time.

"Is it like squaring the circle?" Driftwood finally asked.

"Whatever do you mean?" responded Helena.

"Mathematicians have tried for centuries to find the dimensions of a square and a circle that are exactly equal but have found it to be impossible. They can only relate to each other using a number called pi which starts as 3.141...and goes on and on. It is a non-repeating decimal. We may always get closer to defining pi but there will always be a further unknown to define. Pi will never be complete but every successive version of it leads us closer to squaring the circle. So I have to realize that I will never be perfectly complete, just slowly getting closer."

"Interesting contemplation. Now, I need you to consider how you compose yourself in relation to others."

"What do you mean?"

"You are fairly judgmental."

"How dare you say that?"

"You even sound condemning right now. It is absolutely fantastic that you have beliefs and convictions, Driftwood, and you are very brave in the way you act upon them. However, perhaps if you were more open to look at the many sides of an issue you would find solutions that were less confrontational."

"Yes, but my father –"

"Don't make this about your father. He was someone you didn't even know when you were growing up. Do not let him ruin your life."

"It's not my life I'm worrying about. It's all the people who are being killed in his stupid war."

"There were selfish and stupid wars before Hans Blekansit and there will be more after him as well. You view him as the cause of the planet's ills and really he is more like a symptom. In fact it may even be a mistake to state that the world's problems are like a disease. We are constantly trying to cure things. Our society hopes to exorcize, surgically remove and vaccinate against any problem we face but we never succeed."

"A problem isn't a problem."

"What's that, Driftwood?"

"A problem isn't a problem. I am not good. My father isn't evil. We just are."

"And you are?"

"I am a young girl. I have great power and yet am powerless. I am clumsy and graceful. I believe in myself."

"You are getting close. I want you to look at the light coming towards you."

"From where? The sun?"

"That may be too intense. Try somewhere closer, like the light that is reflecting off of that building."

"I can't see any light. I can only see the building."

"Remember that you are never seeing that building. You are only ever seeing the light that is being reflected off of that building. So now, as you study its windows, doors and floors, I want you to remember that it isn't the building, it's only the light."

"It isn't the building. It's only the light."

"Exactly."

Once she opened herself to learning, Driftwood found herself easily engaged in Helena's mental pursuits.

"Now, I want you to contemplate how everything you see is light reflected off of somewhere. Even the rays of the sun are light that has bounced off a nuclear reaction."

"Bouncy wouncy ouncy," Driftwood mused playfully.

"Perfect free association. Take the light that bounces off of you and remember that it once had form. That it is an altered state of matter but that it can be bent nonetheless."

"Okey dokey."

"Now bend the light around you."

Driftwood easily did exactly as she was instructed. If someone had been looking at her they would have seen her fade away to be replaced by the objects that were behind her.

"Whoa," she gasped as she attempted to look at her hand. "I've become invisible. I used to need a potion to do that."

"And remember that you now know how to do more than become invisible. You can bend light. We are now going to use that skill to journey to the Micromacro where the FSG is."

"Micromacro? FSG?"

"The Micromacro is a sublime-atomic universe. FSG stands for Free Spirit Gathering. Now I want you to look up at those street signs."

Driftwood looked up to see Haight and Ashbury signs sticking out from a street pole that also supported a traffic light and several electrical wires.

"Try to extrapolate the place where the two signs meet. Imagine that infinitesimally small point as growing infinitely large. Let the chasm engulf you."

Driftwood and Helena were being sucked through a very small pinhole in their universe. They emerged into an entirely different version of reality.

"Where are we?" asked a disoriented Driftwood.

"We are in the Micromacro," explained Helena, "where bacteria are gigantic and elephants are miniscule. And all are at peace."

Driftwood looked around and noticed that every creature and entity that she could see was blissfully dancing about. Huge mosquitoes flew in harmony with tiny eagles. A forest of deciduous trees swayed at the base of a massive mushroom. A hippo banged hips with a mouse.

"Welcome, Driftwood," boomed an elegant voice, "to the Free Spirit Gathering."

A woman in majestic robes floated towards them.

"Who are you?" asked Driftwood. "And how did you know my name?"

"I know a great many things about you."

"Why is that?"

"My name is Christine deMage."

"Doesn't mean anything to me."

"I'm Anne Wood's mother."

"What? But that means -"

"Yes, dear. I'm your great grandmother."

Chapter Nineteen

SOLDIER BOY

Del Wood had barely started boot camp when they shipped his platoon up north to the Alert Military Outpost on Ellesmere Island. Shortly after that he found himself on a frontline offensive.

Hans Island boasts an above ocean surface area of approximately 1.3 square kilometres making it the size of a small neighborhood community. Save for the fossils of long ago inhabitants, it is composed almost entirely of gray rock, giving the appearance of a great leviathan rising up from the depths of the deep sea.

When they disembarked, Del, with the other American and Canadian soldiers, established a wall of sandbags on the northwest corner of the island. The Norwegian and Danish soldiers who had journeyed from Greenland had done exactly the same on Hans Island's southwest side. They had been firing bullets at each other for three days. Thor had been giving the Danes an edge. The Norwegian thunder god knocked away the sand bags that shielded Del. He and his foxhole mates scrambled to rebuild their wall. Suddenly, Del felt a sharp pain as he fell to the ground. He wasn't sure if he had been shot or had merely pulled a muscle. He started to breathe heavy. One of the medics came to Del's side and began to administer first aid. Del looked up and marveled at the splendour of the blue sky and how it contrasted to the blunt aggressive noise of bullets firing all around him.

Del squinted his eyes when a small distinct object appeared high above him. He was sure it was a young girl being carried by hundreds of small white birds but it was hard to tell in the sun.

"Good work, birdies," sang Clover. "Now go and try to convince everyone to stop shooting."

The doves landed Clover behind some sandbags that were near Del Wood and flew to the heart of the battle. Half of them flew over to the Dane-Norwegian side. Every bird found the barrel of a gun to land on. Even when the soldiers shook their weapons the doves stayed perched as they stared with soft eyes. The effect was absolute.

There was a ceasefire.

As the soldiers gazed sweetly, the moment initiated in each one of them a memory of tranquil existence like taking a walk in a park or watching a sunset. They lost all ability to fight.

"Those birds are laughing at me," cried Thor, disrupting the peace as he swung at gun barrel after gun barrel.

The birds were forced to scatter. The soldiers remembered that they were under orders to engage the enemy. The melee of ammunition resumed as if it had never stopped.

"Bummer!" spouted Clover.

"At least...you tried something...different," comforted Del in short breaths, "unlike...the rest of us sheep robots."

Clover could see blood spurting from Del's mid-section. The medic was working diligently to patch Del up. Unaware of their connection to each other through Driftwood, Clover felt an unavoidable empathy for Del.

"You're going to be alright," she said to him.
"I don't think so," he gasped.
"Why not?"

"I can't move my legs."

Chapter Twenty

ROOTS

"Once upon a time," began Christine deMage, "there were two men named Gilgamesh and Enkidu."

"Heard it," Driftwood interrupted.

"Not these parts I assure you," Christine continued. "It was generally unknown that Enkidu had fathered a child with the love priestess Shamhat shortly before his death. Shamhat named her son Blekansit."

"Blekansit? Does that mean that the strange electrical being who zapped me is actually my long lost ancestor?"

"Who traveled from the core of the sun outwards through heat and static for thousands of years to be powerfully resurrected."

"Interesting. Gilgamesh has also returned."

"What? Where?"

"At the Order of the Good and True's castle in the centre of Jupiter," Driftwood excitedly explained, feeling proud that she had acquired information that her great grandmother didn't know. "I guess the intense gravitational field is why Gilgamesh was able to attempt a recon-struction of his physical form. When I last saw him he was still working on it but hoping to be solid soon."

"You are right, Driftwood. This is very interesting. I must tell you more of the story. Before Gilgamesh was tamed by the friendship of Enkidu, he was a wicked ruler who did as he pleased, subsequently fathering many unknown children. One of his sons was born by a farm girl who raised the infant with her family. He grew to become a great wizard named Magee."

"Wait a second..."

"If you're asking if Murph, Michael and Marv Magee are descendants of Gilgamesh then the answer is yes."

"Holy Ma-Joley."

"Just wait, dear. There's more. In the early forties, during the heyday of World War II, Malachi Magee, escaped the turmoil of Europe and journeyed with his family to a new world in

America. He had his two children with him, a very young Murph Magee and an even younger Anne deMage. Joining them as well was their mother, myself."

"Magee ... deMage ... "

"We were libertines. I translated Anne's and my surname into the French language of my freedom pursuing ancestors. Our family arrived in New York. Like so many Magees, Malachi was a knight in the Order of the Good and True. He quickly found himself engaging in frequent battles with a despicable corporate wizard named Horatio Blekansit, the ancestor of Heinz, Hans and Harry Blekansit.

"One hot summer day Malachi and I had rented a boat for a family outing. Horatio had rigged the small craft to explode. At the last minute Anne got sick. She and I stayed home while Malachi took Murph out for a sail. The boat exploded, supposedly killing my husband and son. Malachi was able to cast a comprehensive protective spell just in time. The two floated unconsciously in suspended animation for months until they landed ashore, on the other side of the continent, near Squamish, British Columbia. Believing Malachi and Murph to be dead and fearing further aggression from

Horatio, Anne and I moved to Emporia, Kansas, where I raised her as a single mother."

"So that means that-"

"Murph Magee is your great uncle but most importantly because you have both Magee and Blekansit blood you are related to both Gilgamesh and Enkidu."

"Whoa Nelly."

As Driftwood attempted to process the deluge of information that had just been revealed to her, she mindlessly looked around at the many different beings that were dancing at the Free Spirit Gathering. Her awareness anchored when she saw someone who she knew very well. Sharing a boogie with a squirrel god was Sedna the Inuit goddess of the sea. Sedna was doing the twist in a pond while the squirrel god was on a nearby tree branch, kicking up his legs like a Russian dancer. Driftwood ran up to say hello.

"I was wondering when your journeys would finally lead you here, young mortal," greeted Sedna.

"I'm surprised that you're here," said the squirrel god, "considering the trouble that your friends are in."

"What do you mean?" asked Driftwood.

"You haven't heard about the protest riot?"

The events in Ottawa in which the police had turned on the anti-war activists were explained in meticulous detail by the chattering animal deity. Driftwood went back to her great grandmother.

"I have to go," informed Driftwood. "My friends need my help."

"No one really needs help," expressed Christine deMage. "We all are as we are."

"I know, and we must complete ourselves. Helena has been teaching me that. I'm not ready for a full subscription to that philosophy when my friends are being beaten up by police. I don't think helping them is going to prevent them from important self-discovery. It may even help them along the way."

"Before you go I want to introduce you to the Thirteen Chromosomes of the Original Gifted Apewomen."

"The what now?"

"Come with me. It's only in this realm that they could even remotely be a size in which we could see them. Long ago, at the dawn of humanity, there lived a tribe of homo-erectus beings. They were part of one of the early upright species in Africa. A major evolutionary occurrence happened with this tribe. They had thirteen females who were all extraordinarily gifted. They each had a trait of personality that gave inner strength to herself and outer strength to her community. Many people look at things like the wheel and fire as the most important developments in early days but it was really the development of our spirit that has guided us. Their personalities were somehow entwined with their genetic make-up. From each of these foremothers, a distinct chromosome was created to travel dominantly and recessively through civilizations many outer empires. These genes contain many hidden gifts of feminine energy. These chromosomes are the birthplace of our imaginative soul. As well, four of them are on my Free Spirit recreational volleyball team."

Circling about them were thirteen 'X' shaped entities. Their tightly wound nucleotides made them look like they were composed of vibrating springs.

"Wow. What are you called?"

The chromosomes each introduced themselves, their names emanating like a chord from a harp.

"She-Who-Loves."

"She-Who-Listens."

"She-Who-Heals."

"She-Who-Tells-Stories."

"She-Who-Closes."

"She-Who-Connects."

"She-Who-Walks-Tall."

"She-Who-Encourages."

"She-Who-is-Family."

"She-Who-is-Wise."

"She-Who-Weighs-Truth."

"She-Who-Looks-Far."

"She-Who-Completes."

"You are a part of us," they sang in unison, "and we are a part of you."

"Again. Wow. It's very nice to meet you but I really must get going."

"We see you already have the Lingua-Fera."

"Pardon me?"

"You can speak the language of the animals. Would you like to also know the Lingua-Micra?"

"The what?"

"The language of the microscopic. It would allow you to communicate with tiny entities like us but in your realm, however you must shrink yourself for discussion to be possible."

"How do I do that?"

"Complete yourself."

"I'm getting used to that response around here. And of course, I can never fully complete myself so it's a life long process."

"You have learnt much for a young girl. It shows in your wisdom."

"Even if I haven't liked it all the time, I've had a lot of teachers. They all gave me something valuable but there always seemed to be more. All I can say is that I'm game for all that is out there."

"To understand completion one must embrace incompletion. You appear prepared for ways to further connect with the universe. Let these powers that we bestow upon you allow a divide that exists in the physical world to be bridged."

The vibrations of the Thirteen Chromosomes of the Original Gifted Apewomen intensely increased. Driftwood could feel a deep rhythm hum inside her chest. A warmth grew inside of her. She was able to recognize that the chromosomes had given her a great gift.

"Thank you," Driftwood whispered, a bit overwhelmed from the experience.

Gathering her thoughts, she made her way back to Sedna and the squirrel god. She hugged Sedna and then asked the squirrel god to try and get a message to Peter Z. Juice."

"What should I say?" he asked.

"Tell him to have Gilgamesh and Kevin come find me," Driftwood said with a twinkle in her eye. "I have the beginnings of a plan."

Chapter
Twenty-One

DOMINO HURRICANE

The battle on Hans Island, while small in itself, had had devastating ripple effects across the world. When a large powerful country like the United States goes to war, other countries often use it as an excuse to battle their neighbors. Russia attacked Georgia and Estonia. Argentina attacked Chile. China attacked Tibet. Germany attacked Poland. Iraq attacked Iran. Kenya attacked Uganda. There were even reports that the research scientists of Antarctica were getting restless and fighting with each other.

Cultural intolerance had reached an all-time high. People in the United States and Canada had been inundated with anti-Norse

God messages. The breakfast item that people had always called the Danish was now called the Glazed Freedom Bun.

Meanwhile, at the White House in Washington, Hans Blekansit was getting an update on Hans Island.

"Mr. President, some birds caused a minor interference to our offensive," reported the defense minister. A short ceasefire was ended by the actions of Thor."

"Nothing fuels war like a thunder god. However, I think it's time we weakened the Norwegians. Prepare the White House's nuclear missile."

"What nuclear missile?"

Hans pressed a button under his desk. The defense minister looked out the window to see the water in the pool bubble up and drain out as the floor slid open. A rocket carrying a nuclear bomb rose up from below, its top reaching for the sky while chlorinated water dripped dry off its sides.

"Sir, we can't drop a bomb on anyone," protested the defense minister. "With global tensions at an all-time high, it will inevitably start a nuclear war."

"Not if no one else can respond. Enkidu,

blow out the candles," Hans cryptically commanded.

Enkidu jumped into the computer screen on Hans' desk the way one would jump into a diving pool. He surfed effortlessly through the worldwide web. He was able to travel into the secure military operations systems of every other country in the world. He had already done so on numerous occasions since meeting Hans. On these particular visits he disabled every computer and electrical device that each country was using. Radar systems were now useless. Communication had been severly compromised. Launching a missile was now impossible unless you were the United States of America.

"My favorite kind of fight," contemplated Hans. "Fixed."

"Sir, the direction you've taken this government may have disastrous consequences for the world," pleaded the defense minister.

"I don't recall owing the world any favours," defended Hans. "I only joined the government to bend it to my will. And boy does it bend."

"That's just like you, Hans. Selfish to the bone."

"Who's that?"

"Oh, don't tell me you don't recognize the wife you used to hit so affectionately."

"Eva? But you're dead."

"I came back. Now prepare to be haunted, you son of a beast."

Chapter
Twenty-Two

RAYS AND GOONS

"Lichen says she saw you telling those guys to throw rocks at the cops," interrogated Rose as she shook Stormy by the neck. "Is it true?"

"I'm sorry," Stormy cried, his tears a silent confession of guilt.

"Sorry for what?"

"When I was staying with my mother, recovering from the horrors of the Norwegian whaling disaster that I caused by summoning up those angry Norse gods, my brain was shattered by a nervous breakdown. I began to download music to give me something to listen to while I healed. I got arrested for piracy. The government said they would remove all charges if I helped them by spying on peace groups and trying to instigate them towards violence. Apparently, it's one way that the government has been dealing with activists for years. They'll motivate selected members of a group to turn violent and sub-sequently diminish that organization's record. They were very interested when I said that I worked at Camp Magee, because of Driftwood I suspected, but maybe they knew that you would draw us into this kind of thing."

"What can I say?" Rose defended. "I like to get things going, same as you. My way just isn't as secretly manipulative as your's and doesn't result in nearly the same amount of violence."

As Stormy and Rose argued, the conflict between the police and the activists had escalated. People were being handcuffed and dragged off. The military showed up to assist with controlling the crowd. They removed a canvas covering from the back of a truck to reveal a giant ray gun which was quickly turned on and directed at the protesters. Before Stormy and Rose could continue their conversation they both felt a warm glow grow from their insides. It was briefly a pleasant sensation. However, the warmth increased and soon they and everyone else felt like a fire was combusting inside their bodies. People writhed on the ground and screamed in agony. The police retreated with ease and watched as their quarries were painfully subdued.

"That fancy gun sure makes things easier," commented one officer. "Who knew that a ray of light could control a crowd so effectively?"

"If it's light," commented a voice from above, "then it can be bent."

"Ka-Roar!" was squawked.

For her first time Edie managed a graceful landing. Driftwood jumped off.

"Bouncy Wouncy Ouncy," she incanted.

The light that was being shot at the protesters was curved to shine on the police officers. It did not take long for the fire sensation to overtake them. Pretty soon the cops took off their sweaty clothes and ran around screaming.

The military general who watched the events unfold from afar put down his binoculars.

"Release the goons," he commanded.

Driftwood watched as former wrestlers and football players flooded out of the back of some military trucks. The protesters were just recovering from the Pyro-Psychotron.

Driftwood grabbed a megaphone and addressed the crowd.

"Everyone, I know that you've been through a lot and you're about to get the snot beat out of you," she yelled, "but the best way to beat these goons is through non-violence. Unfortunately, if you fight back you will be poorly judged by everyone watching. If you stand tall and let them strike you down you will be sending a strong message. Be brave, be strong, take the brunt and we shall overcome!"

Tide was the first to follow Driftwood's instruction. He was quickly beaten down by a man who used to go by the wrestling name Furious Freedom Fighter. Tide's courage inspired others. Soon everyone stood up boldly, prepared to absorb the blows of the goons.

Driftwood ran over and comforted Tide who was bleeding from his nose.

"Nice to see you," he greeted.

"Nothing would make me happier than to keep holding you," she told him, "but I have to keep going on. I'll come back here after I go help on Hans Island."

"I'll take what I can get."

"You don't have to bleed for me to like you but the roughed up look does kind of suit you."

The brief encounter made Driftwood's heart pound like a bass drum. The two stared into each other's eyes, ignorant of the brutal display around them.

People from all over Canada watched on live television as huge men from the army cracked the skulls of meek activists. The event was quickly carried by international news stations. The general realized that things had gotten out of control.

"Call off the goons," he commanded. "Continuing will only make us look bad."

While the rest of the world was sinking into violent chaos, a tenuous peace reigned, for the time being, on the gentle slopes of Canada's Parliament Hill.

Chapter
Twenty-Three

EVERY WEAPON IS A FOOL IF
YOU VIEW IT RIGHT

On the rocky shores of Hans Island, amidst a flurry of noise and battle, a medic was desperately applying pressure to Del's spinal wound while delicately bracing the fallen boy's back for transport. Clover was holding his hand in an attempt to provide comfort. Bullets were flying as American and Canadian soldiers exchanged ammunition with the Danish and Norwegian military. Thor was striking. An American general was watching the affair from afar.

"Use the Seisma-Whoofer on the thunder god first," he instructed, "and release the circular virus on our enemies."

A crew pulled the canvas cover off to reveal giant speakers supported by elaborate mechanical arms. Two soldiers manipulated various cranks and levers to direct the mesh covered boxes towards Thor, who was continuing his assault on the various sandbag bunkers. As soon as they got a lock the speakers began to vibrate. Thor shook in mid-air, vibrating so much that he dropped his hammer. He began to vomit on the ground.

"This is worse than being laughed at," he groaned.

The speakers were directed at the other front. Walls began to fall exposing many. Canisters were launched. Landing amidst the opposing foxholes and bunkers the small metal containers released a gaseous substance that quickly diffused throughout the air. After a brief symphony of gags and coughs many of the Danish and Norwegian soldiers walked un-controllably and uncoordinatedly in irregular circles.

"Why did they even need me here if they could do that?" contemplated Del in short breaths.

"Why do we need any of this?" responded Clover in sadness.

"I couldn't agree more, dear friend," came a voice from above, "and I see you've met my cousin."

Clover and Del looked up to watch Driftwood and Edie gracefully land.

"What happened, Del?" asked an aghast Driftwood.

"I think I've been shot real bad, Cuz," Del managed to spit out, "but it looks like we're about to be able to shoot us the whole other army."

Driftwood gave Del a tearful hug.

"This is madness," stated Driftwood. "No matter what's happened to you, Del, I can't let my father's weapons continue their torture. What do we have here?"

"It looks like a big earthquake machine and a virus that is making them go in circles," observed Clover.

"Time to use the skills given to me by Helena and the Thirteen Chromosomes of the Original Gifted Apewomen."

"And I heard that something called the Enkidu Beast has thwarted their military radar."

Clover watched as her friend became invisible. Driftwood concentrated and projected her astral self across the island and into one of the metal canisters.

"Hello," Driftwood's miniscule spirit self called out. "Can you hear me, virus?"

"Groovy chick, like dig it. You're totally a phased out tiny magic girl," replied the circular virus.

"Why are you making people go in circles?"

"It's just the way I say, 'hey there let's boogie.'"

"It's quite aggressive."

"Hey what now?"

"Couldn't you affect people much more slowly if you wanted? Try a little patience."

"That's crazy talk. I'm all about the go go go."

"Well, let me break it down for you. If you continue making people lose so much control they will create a vaccine for you. Do you know what that is?"

"What, groovy chick?"

"A vaccine will destroy you."

"Bummer."

"However, if you slow down your process a little bit and are more selective with who you infect we may find an equilibrium."

"I dig, bongo balance and all that."

"Exactly. Some people even kind of enjoy the rhythm of going in circles. You're bound to be able to foster inhabiting the innards of a few hosts."

"Why are you making people go in circles?"

"Gotcha, groovy chick."

"Don't call me chick."

"Gotcha."

Driftwood allowed her astral form to return to her physical body. She turned visible again to watch the outcome of her microscopic diplomacy. The soldiers slowly stopped running in circles. The influence of the virus had assimilated so congruently with the patterns of everyday existence that the impact was now minimal. This allowed the soldiers to run for cover from the Canadian and American fire. It was difficult to do as the Seismi-Whoofers were causing the ground to intensely tremor.

"They've stopped running in circles," commented Clover. "How are you going to stop the earthquakes?"

"I'm going to the core of the Earth," replied Driftwood.

"How are you going to do that?"

"A while back I taught myself how to become nothing. It will allow me to get there. However, I need to make sure I'm grounded when I get there or the intensity of Earth's gravity may cause me to collapse into an infinitely small point."

"Ground yourself? How?"

"Looking at you and Del. Friends and family have been the greatest blessing of the last couple years. Remembering that will get me back."

Driftwood waved a hand in front of her body.

"I am nothing," she incanted.

"Weird," commented Clover as she watched Driftwood sink into the ground.

"I have a feeling the weirdness is just beginning."

Chapter
Twenty-Four

HEART OF A TYRANT

Despite all their efforts, the Secret Service could do nothing to restrain Eva Wood from circling about the ceiling of the oval office.

"Shoot all you want," taunted Eva. "I'm already dead."

"Stand down," commanded Hans. "All you're doing is putting bullet holes in the wall."

"Did you miss me, Hans?"

"You ran away from me when you were pregnant with our daughter."

"After experiencing your abusive nature I died making sure she was born in a place where you couldn't get to her."

"But Driftwood ended up finding me and has antagonized my life ever since."

"If I may interject to reinforce your claim," chimed in the Secretary of Defense, "it appears your daughter has been involved in strengthening the peace protest in Ottawa and is currently thwarting our weaponry in the Hans Island offensive."

"Pardon me?" replied Hans.

"She turned the Pyro-Psychotron's rays onto our forces. The Goons became a public relations disaster. The Circular Virus has somehow been rendered useless. All we have in operation are the Seismi-Whoofers and she has possibly engaged that."

"Well then, it's time for Plan B as in Button."

Hans reached for a button by his desk. Eva unsuccessfully tried to stop him.

"Hans, no!" she screamed as her arms went through her ex-husband.

"Countdown initiated," spoke a loud electronic voice, "Ten minutes until launch."

"With Enkidu halting all mechanical systems of the rest of the world's military it's time for Hans Island to become a cautionary mushroom cloud of a message to everyone else out there. Don't tread on me."

Eva floated to right in front of Hans' face.

"Time to see if there is any empathy in you at all," she cried. "Look into my eyes."

Chapter
Twenty-Five

EARTH AND DRIFTWOOD

Act One Scene One

> DRIFTWOOD and EARTH are standing
> on the creaky wooden stage of an old
> theatre. They both are clad
> in pairs of brown unclean full-body
> long underwear.

EARTH (E) [*singing*]: Hey la la la la la la
la hey now.

DRIFTWOOD (D): I need your help.

EARTH (E): Hey la la la – Oh, hello
human being.

D: I need your help.

E: Who are you?

D: I need your help.

E: I could say the same to you humans.

D: I need your help.

E: Digging into me with your drills and shovels. Cutting down trees that have been more in balance with me than you humans could ever hope to achieve..

D: Whoops. It took me a while to get the hang of this way of speaking. If that's what I'm doing. Why are we both in long underwear? Why do I feel like we're in front of an audience. Who are you?

E: I am known as Earth. And you?

D: I'm Driftwood Ellesmere.

E: Never heard of you. How did you reach me?

D: I sank to the centre. I allowed gravity to collapse me while staying spiritually tethered to Clover and Del. I found myself in a void of endless silence but I assumed your existence. Then I listened.

E: Impressive. Such focused and meditative visits are rare these days.

D: Why are we on a theatre stage? Shouldn't Earth's core be molten magma?

E: You have traveled deeper than that. The stage is merely a symbolic construct that your essence can grasp. You are talking to the sentience of a planet. The reality of that situation would belittle you to insignificance. This form of presentation allows the idea that we are on equal footing to pervade.

D: This isn't like when I was on Jupiter.

E: And how is my sibling doing? It feels like an eternity since we last spoke. Is he still a know-it-all?

D: I didn't talk with Jupiter. I went to
school there and met a ghost named
Gilgamesh who was almost becoming real.
I found out later that I'm related to him.

E: Gilgamesh has returned? May
my surface please be safe.

D: You know Gilgamesh?

E: I will never forget the killing of the great
forest protector Hambaba by the fool-king
Gilgamesh and his beast parallel Enkidu.

D: Their story resonates this far, eh?

E: The ramifications of that tale reverberates
through all I embody. If you are a home to
others it is impossible not to feel bruised
from their episodes. For you humans the
killing of Hambaba was a great victory. To me
it was a tragedy of imbalanced dominance.

D: It was eons before I was born, although
I'm also related to Enkidu so it seems
I am strongly connected to all this.

E: Perhaps I have to fear you as I did them.

D: I've done all I can to save you.

E: Is that why you're here now?

D: I came to try to stop a war.

E: Why would you think I'd care about
your human wars? I often hope that
humanity will wipe itself off my face. The oil
excavation feels like I'm being slowly bled
to death. Am I to become a piece of veal?

D: Until humans find peace we will
be too distracted and manipulated to
address the ravages we inflict upon you.

E: There's iron in your words.
Perhaps I will be able to help.

Chapter
Twenty-Six

HI-YO REDEMPTION, AWAY!

When a person stares into the eyes of a ghost they experience the entire life of the ghost. Hans was reliving the life of Eva Wood in a nanosecond. He saw her born to Rotten and Anne Wood in Emporia, Kansas. He saw Anne lovingly raise her daughter. Hans felt the blows when Rotten Wood struck Eva. It became an even more bizarre experience when he watched Eva meet a younger Hans Blekansit on the show *Fight for Love*. He felt Eva's joy of a new life married to a young businessman. He could see the joy get extinguished as Eva witnessed how cruel Hans had made Harry. He felt the sting when his younger self struck down Eva. This caused Hans to vomit.

"That was horrible," he cried as tears fell down his face for the first time in years.

"And think, Hans," warned Eva, "that was just what you did to me."

"I killed my own mother," Hans confessed in a state of near shock. "I've done such horrible things."

Harry ran into the room.

"Father, what's happened to you?" Harry asked. "You look different."

"Harry, there is so much I want to tell you but most importantly I want you to know that it is important to be good."

"But you always said being good was a weakness that impaired successful business."

"I was wrong. So wrong."

"Missile launch in five minutes," announced a mindless voice.

"Oh no," cried Hans. "Mr. Secretary, announce a ceasefire. Make a peace settlement with Denmark and Norway. Also, stop the missile. It's set to fire itself to Hans Island."

"I'll announce the ceasefire immediately, sir," the Secretary confirmed, "but the missile launch sequence cannot be interrupted."

"What?"

"I believe you put those protocols in place

yourself."

Hans looked out at the missile that was perched in the courtyard.

"I have no time," he contemplated. "Harry, be good."

Hans ran out the door of the oval office. His guards followed him. Hans jumped onto the rocket just as its boosters fired up. He was prying open a side panel just as the missile fired into the air.

"Well done, Hans," said the ghost Eva. "You just may make your daughter proud yet."

Chapter
Twenty-Seven

· FORGIVENESS

Driftwood floated up to the surface of Hans Island.

"I am something," she incanted.

Although the Seismi-Whoofers were still operating, the earthquakes had stopped. Driftwood's conversation with Earth had payed off. Now she just had to deal with the fact that everyone was firing guns at each other.

"Cease fire!" yelled an American officer in miraculous answer to that problem. "The President has called off the war."

Similar announcements were being made on the other side of the island. For a moment all that could be heard was the chirping of the birds that had traveled with Clover followed by the exuberant cheers of soldiers who no longer had to kill or be killed.

"No time for celebrations," the officer continued. "We must evacuate immediately. A nuclear bomb from Washington is headed directly for us."

Two soldiers carried Del away on a stretcher. Clover found herself going with them, feeling a quick connection to the wounded boy she had just met. She hadn't let go of Del's hand since meeting.

Driftwood jumped onto Edie the Eaderion and held tightly to fur and feather. The two flew high into the air.

"Let's find that bomb before it reaches us, Edie!"

"Ka-Wow!"

The missile that had left Washington was an experimental nuclear weapon that could travel three times faster than the speed of sound and around the whole planet if need be. It had to travel over about a quarter of the Earth to reach Hans Island. The journey would take about three hours. It had finished its second hour by the time Driftwood encountered it.

"Here it comes, Edie! Get your claws ready!"

As the missile flew past them, Edie pounced

onto the projectile and gripped it tight with her eight strong paws. Driftwood was surprised by what she saw. A man with half his flesh burnt off was pulling out wire after wire from an open panel on the side of the rocket bomb. Further shock overwhelmed Driftwood when she realized the man destroying the bomb was her father, the nemesis of her life.

"Disengage, damn you!" Hans yelled.

Sparks flew out of the panel burning Hans even more. The flames that emitted from the boosters extinguished themselves. The rocket started to fall straight down.

"OVERRIDE SUCCESSFUL," spouted an electronic voice.

Driftwood grabbed the weakened body of her father in her arms. Edie flapped with great effort. The rocket landed inert against a gravelly mountain slope in northern Quebec.

"Driftwood, is that you?" Hans gasped. "Did it all work out?"

"The bomb was stopped if that's what you mean."

"At least I did one good thing in my life."

"Hans? Father? Dad? Hang in there, Sir. If it helps you find strength in the moment...I forgive you."

"To be forgiven is fine and dandy, daughter,

but it does nothing to remove the regret I feel for the life I've led. You have been wise to be good."

Hans let out a cough full of tightened strength, unrestrained pain and fluid dynamics. Immediately afterwards his whole body relaxed and went limp.

Scouting the vast countryside for the Red Cross symbol, carrying her crew to safety, Edie swooped and landed in front of a medi-centre in Val-Paradis, Quebec. Nurses and medics rushed out to treat Hans as he was directed to the emergency surgical room. When the doctor arrived, Hans was quickly and irrefutably declared dead-on-arrival.

Driftwood found herself crying over the death of the one person in the world she had forever hated. Stumbling out of the clinic she found solace support by leaning against the remains of an old washed-up-by-the-river-during-some-unforeseen-time log. The flat cut-off part was both strong and flaky.

Picking at the dry and brittle rings gave indescribable comfort.

Dripping tears and still in a state of shock, Driftwood got on her mystic steed to continue her quest for global salvation.

Chapter
Twenty-Eight

OH BROTHER

Rose, Tide, Glacier, Lichen, Wave and even Stormy had continued their vigil on the steps of Canada's parliament with the other activists. Without police interference they were able to calmly gather. However, they were aware of the global events as they watched the international news on Lichen's wireless laptop. The violence on Hans Island had stopped but the rest of the world had slipped into chaos. After Enkidu had disabled the electronic capability of every other country's military, there had been a variety of brutal outcomes. Due to their new vulnerability, every nation was on a heightened state of alarm, fearing the invasion of their neighbor. Some countries slipped into anarchy. Others declared marshal law and turned on their citizens.

"Holy Ma-Joley," exclaimed Rose. "We're at peace now but the rest of the world is still in bad shape."

"It's time we did something about that," Rose heard a familiar voice say from above.

Landing beside the activists, Driftwood jumped off of Edie and gave Rose a warm embrace. When she was finished, Tide had navigated himself to be the next recipient. Everyone watched with interest as the two hugged for quite a long time.

"Get a room," joked Wave.

Everyone laughed while Driftwood and Tide stared deeply at each other. A rope ladder lowered itself between their gazes. Driftwood looked up to see Peter Z. Juice climbing down with Kevin and Gilgamesh above him.

"Finally," she said.

"We got here as soon as that squirrel god got his message to me," explained Peter. "I understand that you've had quite a few interesting conversations since we last talked. How is my sibling doing?"

"Who's your sibling?"

"Earth."

"But that means..."

Driftwood contemplated Peter Z. Juice's name to a point of revelation.

"Are you the planet Jupiter?" she asked.

"At your service," Peter spoke as he bowed. "At everyone's service on most days. The Order of the Good and True has tried to help humanity care for Earth since the first caveman cut down a tree."

"I guess I shouldn't have given you guys such a hard time," spoke yet another voice that came from above.

Old Bart, Hermit the Laughing Man and Anne Wood floated down on old pieces of newspaper. Driftwood was happy to see her many relatives but was sad to tell them about Del. After calming Anne Wood down, she continued with her announcements.

"Grandma Wood, do you see that old man with my friends?"

"Yes, dear."

"His name is Murph Magee. He's your brother."

Driftwood introduced Anne to Murph and explained how she had met their mother's spirit in the MicroMacro realm.

"Uh, Drifty?" interrupted Rose. "I hate to remind you but the whole world is immersed in terror right now."

"Right, and I even have a plan," announced Driftwood. "Lichen, can my friend Kevin use your laptop?"

"Of course," said Lichen. "Anything to help."

"Kevin, I want you to use the internet to try to contact the Enkidu Beast that has infected the global security systems."

"What should I say when I find him?" Kevin asked.

"Tell him Gilgamesh says hello," Driftwood clarified.

It didn't take Kevin long to find Enkidu on the worldwide web. Moments later, the electrical creature leapt out of the laptop screen.

"So, Gilgamesh, we meet again after all these years," sparked Enkidu. "Let's see if you're as strong as I've become."

Enkidu blasted Gilgamesh with a bolt of energy. Struggling to even exist out of the dense gravity of Jupiter's core Gilgamesh let the energy easily pass right through him.

"Still as wild as ever, mate," Gilgamesh laughed. "I may be almost entirely a ghost but I have power where it counts."

Gilgamesh lunged towards Enkidu and

concentrated enough to make one of his hands solid. Enkidu was struck down by the fist.

"Stop it!"yelled Driftwood. "You guys were best friends. Why do you fight now?"

"He let me die," explained Enkidu.

"This is how I play with friends," defended Gilgamesh.

"The two of you," Driftwood commanded, "look into my eyes."

When the two of them did as requested, they experienced all the history that connected them to Driftwood. They saw the generations of descendents that led to Hans Blekansit and Eva Wood meeting and thus bringing the blood of Enkidu and Gilgamesh together. They saw the violence that their descendents had inflicted on one another ultimately leading up to the abusive relationship of Driftwood's parents. They saw the amazing and heroic person Driftwood had become in the modern age.

"We are an old story," Enkidu realized.

"Your's is a tale for the now of things," Gilgamesh told Driftwood. "It is more important that we learn from you than the other way around."

"I'm flattered and mostly just relieved that you aren't trying to hurt each other anymore. Now, Tide, did you guys bring your instruments?"

"You bet we did."

"Good. Now, Edie, I want you to eat Lichen's laptop," Driftwood instructed.

"Ka-Yeah!"

"Kevin, I want you to work with Edie and Enkidu and get my friends' music to be played across every possible medium in the world."

"Cool, Drifty, I get it" chimed in Rose.

"Get what?" asked Glacier.

"She's creating a global dance party."

Chapter
Twenty-Nine

THE BOOGIE SHALL SET YOU FREE

Yevgeneh Piotrovich and Zsolt Sabach were strangling each other on the Margit Bridge in Budapest. They hadn't even known each other until, only minutes earlier, Zsolt had stepped on Yevgeneh's toe. The world events had driven them both to a state of total paranoia and they found themselves mindlessly at each other's throats. From a car radio they could suddenly hear infectious music. It was coming from all of the car radios and could even be heard playing from a restaurant on nearby Margit Island. Yevgeneh and Zsolt found themselves listening and calming down. They both felt an overwhelming sense of peace and joy. The two were soon linking elbows and dancing a wondrous jig.

All over the planet people danced liked there was no tomorrow. For some reason, the Camp Magee band's music was exactly what every country needed to relax and retreat. It prompted people from Serbia to El Salvador to run out to the streets and dance with their neighbours. All guns were put down. All tensions diffused. Very shortly people began playing their own music to fill every street in the world with its own distinct jubilation. Every living soul got to experience it. It was the world's first global dance party. For three days and nights the energetic celebration went on and on. People then slept for nearly forty-eight hours. Following that, things generally returned to normal but without most of the military tensions that had existed previously.

Driftwood and her friends also returned to their various homes, both old and new.

Anne Wood decided that she needed a change of pace and moved to Ellesmere Island. There she would help Old Bart, Wilson and Clara at the Toque and Mitt Inn.

Rotten Wood was sent to prison for the malicious assault of his wife. He soon died from a heart attack he had during a mandatory

*All over the planet people danced
liked there was no tomorrow.*

exercise session.

Hermit the Laughing Man resumed his identity as Heinz Blekansit and took over the business operations of Great Blekansit Products. It became his intention to shift the goals of the company towards noble activities. He did so with the help of Helena Blekansit. They both did their best to teach Harry how to be a responsible and caring businessman.

Peter Z. Juice and Kevin returned to the Order of the Good and True's headquarters and school in the centre of Jupiter. Kevin finished at the top of his class that year. He credited his time with Driftwood as giving him unique insight into creative thinking.

Del Wood went through extensive rehabilitation but never regained the use of his legs. He became a well known folk singer that sang songs speaking out against war and other forms of oppression.

Like Del, both Gilgamesh and Enkidu entered show business and became a slapstick comedy act.

Hans Blekansit was given a quiet, anonymous funeral in Val-Paradis. Eva Wood, who was impressed with her husband's change of heart, led his ghost on a journey to the Free

Spirit Gathering.

When still in Ottawa, Murph Magee approached Driftwood and presented her with a special offer.

"You have truly demonstrated that you are an independent thinker, capable of great learning," observed Murph.

"I like the knowledge I gained from both the Regimental Conservatory and the Free Spirit Gathering but didn't find myself comfortable in either of those environments," explained Driftwood.

"I've spoken with my grandson, Marv or Swamp as you know him, and he is interested in turning part of the camp into a school for magic."

"Really?"

"How would you like to be one of the main teachers?"

"Sounds like a plan."

All of the other counselors joined Driftwood as they returned to Camp Magee to launch its new and exciting program. Even Stormy was forgiven and brought on to teach Mythic Summonings.

The day before the first set of magic students were to arrive, Driftwood found herself lying alone in the middle of the main field, meditating and watching clouds change shape. Tide came and sat down beside her. Things had happened so fast with launching the magic camp that they'd barely had time to talk.

"You really saved the day this time, Driftwood," he commented.

"We all saved the day," returned Driftwood. "You, the other counselors, even my father. In fact, everyone who danced around the planet saved the day."

"Anyways, since the world is safe for the time being and we don't start work until tomorrow, I was wondering something?"

"What is it, Tide?"

"Would you like to go on a picnic with me, like as a date?"

"You know something?" Driftwood replied as she grabbed Tide's hand. "That sounds like it would be a lot of fun."

The End

Recycled
Supporting responsible use
of forest resources
www.fsc.org Cert no. SGS-COC-003153
© 1996 Forest Stewardship Council

Marquis Book Printing Inc.

Québec, Canada

2010

Printed on Silva Enviro which contains 100% recycled post-consumer fibre,
is EcoLogo, Processed Chlorine Free and manufactured using biogas energy.